Frail and Delicate Princess

"Princess Bianca rules, in every way! This tale of intrepid discovery and determination will delight young readers and will dare those who deal with the dragons of self-doubt, frustration, and bullying to step out and challenge those menaces to a duel."

New England Children's Book Review
Listed as a "Favorite"

"Spry and charming . . . exquisitely characterized animials. Runs to surprising depths, and Sammy the donkey will live long in young memory. Bianca, all told, is a memorable middle-grade heroine."

Kirkus Reviews

"Dendler's writing is smooth and accessible with small details of lavish castle living and fairy tale adventure that readers on the younger end of the middle-grade spectrum are likely to savor. Princess Bianca--as she proves herself to be brave and independent rather than coddled and frail--will be a strong draw for reluctant readers."

BookLife

Books Worth Devouring

StoryMonsters.com

Story Monster Approved!

Kid Reviewed. Kid Approved!

Books by Meg Welch Dendler

Cats in the Mirror Series

Book 1: *Why Kimba Saved The World*
Book 2: *Vacation Hiro*
Book 3: *Miss Fatty Cat's Revenge*
Book 4: *Slinky Steps Out*

And the Companion Books to the Series
Max's Wild Night
Dottie's Daring Day

Also by Meg Dendler:
Bianca: The Brave Frail and Delicate Princess
At the Corner of Magnetic and Main

Bianca:

Frail and Delicate Princess

by

Meg Welch Dendler

SERENITY MOUNTAIN PUBLISHING
Springdale, Arkansas

Published by Serenity Mountain Publishing
Springdale, Arkansas

Bianca: The Brave Frail and Delicate Princess

Printed in the United States of America

www.megdendler.com

First Edition

ISBN: 978-0692920411
ISBN: 0692920412

Cover art by Callista Rose Dendler.
Cover design by Kelsey Rice.

To Mr. Lenkart and my fifth grade class
Booker T. Washington Elementary School
Champaign, Illinois
Where Princess Bianca began her brave life

Chapter 1

Flames leapt from the dragon's golden jaws and blazed through the sky above the forest.

Princess Bianca didn't flinch. Her tiny feet slipped around inside the stolen boots, but she planted them firmly on the mossy ground and stared straight up past the bronze, armored belly of the beast that threatened her kingdom and every living being for miles around.

As the last flames blew away on the breeze, the dragon glared down at her. Smoke billowed from his nostrils with every breath. People usually ran in fear at the very sight of him, but this girl in ill-fitting peasant clothes stood her ground and planted her hands on her hips.

"Where is my father?" she demanded. "Where is the king? Where are the knights who rode with him?"

The dragon bent his mammoth head down until he hovered only inches above her. Tendrils of smoke swirled around her dark, curly hair as he chortled with amusement.

"I would imagine the same thing happened to them as has befallen every other knight and king who rides against me."

He poofed a quick flame above her head as an example and tipped his face so they were now eye to eye.

"Then you are going to be one sorry dragon."

One Month Earlier

Princess Bianca had never been so bored in all thirteen years of her cushy, royal existence. And that was saying something. Most of the days of her life in the Kingdom of Pacifico blended together and rambled on and on with a sameness that could numb the sharpest spirit. But now that she was getting too old for tutors, there were not even those dull lessons to look forward to.

Princess Bianca knew she shouldn't complain. She had everything in the world she would ever possibly need. Her father, King Dominic, loved her to the point of smothering. And she was told daily that everyone in the kingdom thought she was the most wonderful princess who had ever lived.

Every afternoon, at precisely one o'clock, she would wave to her subjects from a window up high in her castle tower, and they would cheer and wave back.

"She is so beautiful and dainty," the men would say. "We are so lucky to have such a perfect example of princessness in our kingdom."

"Never a hair out of place," the women would say with a sigh. "Constantly smiling and so gracious."

Bianca's bedroom was always full of flowers that were left on the castle steps by children—and sometimes even by bold young men, who hoped to gain her attention in a different way altogether. The boys, however, were wasting their time. Nanny and the multitude of servants who dealt with bringing the flowers to Bianca's room never mentioned a single name. Cards bearing declarations of love were burned on the kitchen hearth.

"Stupid boys," Nanny would snipe. "Nothing better to do with their time and energy than pile flowers on our delicate princess, who will never choose her own husband anyhow."

Cook would nod and agree.

Princess Bianca could be admired from afar, but not one of those young men would ever get within one hundred feet of her.

"Their parents should have better control of them and get them out in the fields for some useful work," Cook would say as she stirred whatever pot of deliciousness she had created for the next royal meal.

Standing above the daily fray of flowers and adoration, the princess was grateful that the townspeople loved her. She knew not every kingdom had loyal subjects. But what would really bring her joy was to throw open the castle doors, frolic through the green grass, and kick up dirt on the dusty paths with those same children who flocked to her window every afternoon.

However, that was not allowed.

Not ever.

From the time the princess was born, everyone had said that she was so frail and so delicate that she must be protected diligently. Her mother, Queen Ariana the Kind, had not survived the birth, and Bianca had nearly joined her in the grave. For weeks, the nurses had stayed by her side every moment and documented each cough and sneeze. Then those weeks extended into months . . . and into years.

King Dominic was terrified that he would lose his beloved daughter to illness or her own frailty, so he kept her hidden away inside the strong castle walls.

The doctor had stressed how weak she was at birth, and the king would not take any chances. Of course, that was thirteen years ago, but her father never overcame his fears or his safeguarding of each second of her life.

Never, not for an instant, was she allowed to meet other children. Playing with one was out of the question. Who knew what kinds of diseases they carried?

Never, not for even one brief moment, had she been allowed outside the castle fortifications. The gray stone walls of the enormous fortress had been built by her ancestors over many centuries. It was like a city unto itself, designed for safety and protection from attack. For Bianca, the castle had become a shield from the outside world—and a prison she couldn't escape.

Princess Bianca could dream of what grass felt like, but she had never touched it. Not once. She could wander around within the castle walls to the stable and such, but there was nothing there but hard-packed dirt paths. The daily flowers in her room were the only bit of nature she was allowed. That tradition of bringing her flowers had started with her dangerous birth as gifts and well-wishes from the kingdom, and her father had allowed it to continue.

Carefully selected tutors had been brought into the castle to teach her to read, do math, learn to speak five useless languages for countries she would never visit, play the piano, create elaborate needlework, and ensure that she was the most accomplished young lady in the kingdom. And she certainly was because most girls didn't have eight hours a day to devote to such tasks.

The king was delighted and proud.

But the princess was lonely and bored.

No matter what was said about her, the princess did not *feel* frail or delicate. She had heard the stories of her birth and the doctor's warnings—over and over and over—but none of it seemed a part of her own lungs and heart and arms and legs. It was as if they were fussing about a stranger she had never met. Many times she had tried to get her father to let her venture outside the castle. Maybe just for a walk or to ride a horse quietly through the woods, surrounded by soldiers.

"But what if you fall off?" the king would wail. "What if there is an angry bumblebee or a rain storm or a cold wind, or what if . . . ?"

Her father always had a "what-if" for any plea she made. Eventually, the princess had just given up, resigned to the fact that her life would be dull and sheltered and protected forever.

But when no one was looking, she would sneak away and race through the quiet hallways of the castle. She would pull off her fancy shoes, hike up her frilly dress, and take the stairs two at a time. And there were thousands of stairs. She would sneak the swords off the displays of suits of armor and pretend to fight invading forces and murderous monsters. Imaginary warriors and mighty dragons would drop in her path as she wielded the sword bravely through the hallways and up and down the staircases.

Of course, she always won.

Then she would fix her hair, straighten her dress, put her dainty shoes back on, and return to Nanny and her maids as though nothing had ever happened.

But that day, the day she was the most bored she

had ever been in her entire sheltered existence, there appeared to be no escape from her tedious captivity. The castle was full of people, so nowhere would be truly safe for running and playing. And Nanny surely wouldn't let her get near that many citizens anyhow. Coming into contact with a person from outside the castle was avoided at all costs for the Frail and Delicate Princess Bianca. Nanny would have her guard up and probably even skip her afternoon nap just to keep an eye on the princess.

To make matters worse, it was raining for the third day in a row, and no one even showed up to greet her at one o'clock because the mud was so deep.

Looking out over the murky courtyard on that rainy day, that was the most depressed that Bianca had ever been. The smiling faces of her townspeople were one of the few bright spots in her mundane life, but that day she was deprived of them as well. She flopped down on her very pink fluffy bed in her very pink frilly room and sighed.

Since the castle was too busy for her to sneak off and fight imaginary monsters, she pulled a book of fairy tales from her bedside table and propped herself up to read her favorites . . . again. Books were another bright spot she could always count on. She could lose herself there in all the adventures she would never have. If only her own kingdom could be so exciting and full of magic, like fairies and dragons and witches.

And so that was how Bianca expected her life to continue.

Day after day.

Year after year.

But an unexpected and unwelcome visitor to her kingdom would upend it all.

Unknown to Princess Bianca, there was a dark reason all the townspeople had come to the castle that day. For weeks, horrible news had spread like a thick winter fog from the outlying farms to the villages and to the king himself.

At first, the king brushed it off as only a rumor, but now there were too many frightened citizens to ignore. He was forced to face the fact that the terrible stories of impending devastation and ruin must be true. The invader even the strongest and bravest king feared with his whole being was heading their way.

It would prove without a doubt that Bianca's kingdom was more magical than she had been led to believe.

Chapter 2

The whole castle was abuzz with predictions of the kingdom's approaching doom.

At first, Bianca didn't understand what the fuss was all about. There were whispers in the hallways and tears from some of the servants, but everyone grew quiet the moment the princess approached. They could pretend all they wanted. She was smart enough to know when something was being hidden from her. It had been going on her entire life. Her father had insisted she be sheltered from any news that might distress her, so she had grown accustomed to the shifty eyes and cut-short conversations of castle staff trying to keep her in the dark.

Normally, it wasn't a big problem because nothing much happened in her kingdom. Sometimes farmers fought over who owned what cow or argued about tools that were borrowed and not returned. The king and his advisors would step in to help negotiate a truce or solution if it got out of hand. There wasn't much crime. Townsfolk all knew each other too well. Their lives went on much like Bianca's, the same from day to day to day.

The last few days had been different, however. The princess sensed it. Nanny kept a straight face and pretended all was well, but Bianca had heard frantic whispers on the other side of her door and caught the frightened expressions of the maids in the hallway when her door opened and shut.

Something very scary was afoot.

Bianca had gotten quite stealthy at creeping around and finding out castle secrets. She could even niggle information out of Nanny, but this was different. Nanny's lips were sealed. The usual gossip among the maids was now whispered. Doors that were normally left ajar just enough for a sneaky princess to spy were now shut tight. Bianca felt the tense atmosphere in the stones around her.

This secret was a big one.

As she often did, the princess decided to tiptoe to her father's Hall of Council and peek through the doorway. Anything worthy of note in the kingdom ended up being discussed there eventually.

Eavesdropping at the Council Room door was how she had learned about a food shortage when she was eight years old. After heavy rains, mold had destroyed a large portion of the crops. There was food rationing, and many families barely survived that year.

Bianca, of course, never missed a meal.

Listening at that door was also how she had learned that her father would select her husband. Names and pedigrees had been bandied about as long as she could remember. Princess Bianca would someday marry a strong, noble hero of royal blood, who would take over when her father was old and gray. His own father would have trained him properly. This husband would care for everything in the kingdom, including

Bianca.

She had never met any of the young men in question. Marriage was many, many years away, so Bianca just enjoyed listening to various royal fathers make a case for their most magnificent sons while her father listened doubtfully. She could imagine him wondering: Who would ever be good enough for his kingdom and his precious daughter?

Spying at the Council Room door had provided her with the answers to castle secrets most of her life, but now more important events were unfolding than royal weddings or even famines. She was certain of it.

So that night, while Nanny slept, Bianca snuck through the castle to the Hall of Council. There, the bravest knights in the kingdom were arguing about what should be done. Table tops were pounded by battle-worn fists. Swords swung in the air. And she could hear words like "fire-breathing" and "monster" and "end of our glorious kingdom" echo through the great room. The creature had been spotted at the far eastern edge of the realm, and he was surely headed for the castle at that moment.

When the truth hit her, Bianca covered her mouth

to muffle the instinctive gasp that escaped. There was only one kind of fire-breathing monster the princess had ever heard of.

Her father and his knights were talking about a dragon.

That's all it could possibly be.

A cold chill ran along her spine and made the hair on the back of her neck stand up.

A dragon? In Pacifico? But dragons aren't real.

Before she had time to think about it more or hear her father's plans, Nanny discovered her listening intently at the door. She had awoken to find the princess missing and had begun a frantic search of the castle. Upon discovering the child overhearing such horrible news, Nanny squealed in distress.

"Oh, Young Miss, you must not listen to such things! It will be the end of you for sure, such a shock."

"But Nanny," she protested as she was led away by the arm, "I am the princess. I am first in line to take the throne of this kingdom. I have to know what is going on."

"Oh, don't be silly, Bianca," Nanny scolded. "The

king has matters in hand now."

"But what about when I am queen? I will need to make decisions to protect my people."

"Your husband will handle any danger to this kingdom. That is man's work. Your job is to be lovely and stay healthy and safe. You know the rules your very own father has established. Be a good girl. Come back to bed, and let the men handle this. What can you possibly know about the problems they are discussing?"

Nanny herded her away from the agitated knights and back to her own very safe and very pink bedroom. Bianca sighed and flopped onto her enormous soft and fluffy bed, pink gauzy fabric billowing up around her. She wanted to ask Nanny if dragons were real, but she knew she'd never get a straight answer.

A dragon? In her kingdom? There was no other explanation for what she had heard in the Council Room.

Dragons were real. And one was headed their way.

She felt her arms go all goosebumpily. In her fairy tale books, dragons were terrifying and cruel and merciless. All was left in char and ruin. What could her father and his knights possibly do to stop that from happening to their kingdom?

No one slept much that night.

The rain had finally ended, so before the first light of day, everyone in the castle began preparations for a dragon hunt.

Chapter 3

At dawn, King Dominic arrived at Bianca's door to say goodbye. She woke to hear him whispering with Nanny at the doorway. In the dim light, she noticed he was dressed in travel clothes, instead of his normal royal attire. Her heart sank.

"Father," she whispered, "are you leaving?"

The king sat on the edge of her bed, and his shoulders slouched.

"Nanny tells me that you already know about the dragon."

"Yes," she admitted, surprised to be provided with such easy proof that her fears were well-founded.

Dragons are real. Dragons are real. She still couldn't quite wrap her thoughts around that.

"And you know it is my duty to protect this kingdom from anything that threatens it."

"Yes, Father," she said, pulling the pink covers up to warm her from the sudden chill she felt. "But how can you conquer a dragon? Has it ever been done? I mean, in *real life*."

"Don't you worry yourself about that now," he said, patting her knee. "You are safe here with Nanny and the castle guards. Your tower is the most secure place in the whole kingdom. I'll be back before you know it. There's nothing to fuss about."

He kissed her on the top of the head as he rose to leave, but Bianca realized from the shifting of his eyes that he was not as confident about his own safety as he wanted her to be.

"I love you, Bianca," he said from the doorway.

"I love you too, Father."

Nanny shut the door behind her and the king, but

Bianca could still hear her muffled sobs as the king's heavy boots echoed away down the hallway.

The princess lay in bed and stared at the ceiling for a few minutes before she was ready to face the day. Bored and lonely was one thing. Terrified and helpless were feelings she had never experienced before.

Within the hour, King Dominic and all the bravest knights and soldiers in the kingdom rode off in a great parade with cheering and confetti. Once again, the whole kingdom had known something before Bianca, and they were ready and waiting to send off their ruler in grand style. Surely, the army would kill the dragon, or at least scare him back out of the kingdom. Everyone was confident.

Bianca watched from her window as her father and his knights and the soldiers rode off into the distance. She didn't turn away until the last speck of blue on the last soldier's uniform dissolved into the horizon.

The Frail and Delicate Princess Bianca may have been young. She may have been sheltered. She may not have understood how the world worked. But she did understand danger. Her father and Nanny saw imagined danger for her around every corner and in every moment of every day. Staring after the army, Bianca realized that her father had just marched into serious danger. Real danger, not the delusions of danger she had faced before.

A sickly feeling settled in her stomach. It was sort of like how she had felt years ago knowing there was not enough food in her kingdom, but this was much worse. Back then, she knew there would be enough rations for everyone to survive. This time, there was no assurance at all. She knew she would not feel at peace again until her father and his fighting forces marched back through the castle gates and the dragon was gone from her realm.

Waiting helplessly would be the hardest part. But what else could she do?

A week later, the king had not returned.

Each morning, Bianca threw open her window and strained her eyes to the end of the village road, looking for any sign of her father. Maybe a lone soldier bringing back news. But every morning she saw nothing but the farmers and the townsfolk going about their normal business.

Soon, there were no farmers either.

Are they hiding at home, or have they run from the kingdom altogether? she wondered.

Two weeks later, and still not a word.

One afternoon at one o'clock, when Bianca went to the window to greet her adoring fans, only two small children stared up at her. A few dozen men and women scurried around the village square, not even looking in her direction. She blew a kiss to the children, and they blew her kisses in return before each was scooped up by an anxious parent, oblivious to the princess watching them.

She understood their distraction. What good was a silly princess cloistered in a castle when the king and all his knights might be dead and a ravenous dragon could drop from the sky at any moment?

Bianca sank onto a giant, pink-cushioned chair in hopelessness. The flowers that normally filled her room had become more and more scarce, and the few that remained were wilted and dying. Who cared about flowers when the end was near?

Thinking about the sweet faces of the children who shared the flowers of their fields with her, Princess Bianca's chest swelled with pride and a determination she had never experienced before.

King Dominic was not there. He might never return. She had tried not to think about that possibility, but it had become too obvious to ignore. Along with that knowledge came another realization that weighed on her even more.

"I am now the one responsible for protecting the kingdom," she whispered to herself.

And she was right.

The Frail and Delicate Princess Bianca was now the one responsible for dealing with the dragon.

She knew how the Kingdom of Pacifico was run. If the king was gone, she was in charge. It had never happened before, but that was the royal order of things. The king's brother—Uncle Frederick, the duke—lived in the castle too, but he was never in on big meetings or important decisions. He preferred to bother Cook for extra snacks, ride his fancy horses around the countryside, and be generally silly and useless. Nanny had once called him a flibbertigibbet. Since the first news of the dragon, he had mostly just hidden in his room, hoping it would all go away. Duke Frederick had no interest in being responsible for anything, ever, and everyone knew the king never planned on putting him in charge.

Of course, the king never really expected Bianca to be in charge of anything either. When he left on the dragon hunt, he'd expected Nanny to be in charge until he returned. She was always very efficient and sufficiently bossy.

The king had done nothing to prepare his only daughter to rule the kingdom, but that didn't mean she hadn't done plenty of listening and learning on her own. Bianca was a princess, and she took that duty seriously.

And she was not as frail and delicate as everyone believed.

The castle was in a state of chaos. And in that chaos, Nanny and the servants (the ones who were left) stopped fussing so much about the princess.

They had bigger fish to fry. More important and more immediate worries. The staff expected she would simply hide in her room in terror.

But the princess was not planning on hiding.

As the days wore on into the third week with still no word of the hunting party, her heart grew bolder and bolder. It ached for her father, the only parent she had ever known. But something else stirred too.

All of that battling pretend monsters in the castle hallways would come in handy now. The Frail and Delicate Princess Bianca was going to open those castle doors. She would step out on her own and take charge of the situation.

Standing in her tower window, looking out over the farms and villages and fields that she had gazed at her entire life, Bianca knew she would do her duty as Princess of Pacifico. It was her birthright, and she wouldn't pass it off to anyone else. Not a spoiled prince from another kingdom that she was expected to marry someday, not her flaky uncle, and certainly not a monstrous dragon.

She would discover what had happened to the king

and his army.

She would find the dragon.

She would go alone.

She would be brave.

Chapter 4

That night, while Nanny and the rest of the castle were still asleep, Bianca put her plan into action. Her heart pounded in her chest like she had run up a flight of steps, and her stomach felt queasy. It was that hope-I-don't-get-caught feeling she knew intimately, but that night it was doubled, if not tripled. She tiptoed so carefully not even the castle mice would hear.

She left a note on her Uncle Fredrick's desk to explain her plan and tell him that he was in charge until she got back. He had always been a bit dotty, but she hoped he would take the job seriously. At least there weren't many people left to worry about at the castle itself anymore. Most folks had scattered to the west, as far from the dragon as possible.

Slyly gathering food and what supplies she imagined she might need, Bianca slipped into some plain clothes and boots she borrowed from the abandoned servants' quarters, grabbing a change of clothes as well. Trying to be practical, she chose pants with suspenders to hold them up. She'd never worn pants before, and something about donning them made her feel even more rebellious. Bianca hid her frilly, pink princess clothes under a pile of laundry.

Taking stock of her stash of bread, cheese, jerky, fruit, and vegetables, she wondered if it would be enough. She assumed she would be able to restock her food at some point in a store or village along the way. She could carry only so much at one time and only so long before the food would spoil. It would have to do.

"Now, how am I going to carry all the things I might need for several days on the road?" she wondered aloud, staring at the pile. "I'm going to need some help."

Holding a lantern in front of her, the princess

headed to the stables in the hope of finding an animal who could help her manage the burden of food, clothes, and bedding. She was stronger than anyone suspected from running through the castle when no one was looking, but walking for miles each day seemed like enough of a challenge without a load on her back.

Though she had never been allowed to touch the horses, Bianca had spent many hours wandering through the castle stables. She had a vague idea about how to put on a saddle and bridle from watching the groomers at work. That night, however, was not the moment to try to figure it all out. And she had no idea about how to ride. The knights and soldiers had probably taken most of the horses with them anyhow.

Searching past all the empty stalls, Bianca found one lone, gray donkey. He was asleep standing up, head hung low, with one back foot crooked.

He stirred at the light filtering through the slats of his stall, ambled over to the gate, and gazed up at the girl with his big, brown eyes.

"You have the longest eyelashes I have ever seen," she said in wonder. "How have I never noticed you before?"

Breaking her father's rule for "established stable-time behavior," she reached over the wooden gate and rubbed the white patch on the donkey's forehead. It felt rougher than she had expected, but it was also warm and alive and full of energy. She could sense it emanating from him.

"Sammy." She read a nameplate attached to the fence. "Looks like they left you behind too. Interested in a little adventure?"

The donkey snorted and tossed his head. Then he inched closer to the gate for another pat.

Bianca took this as a *yes.*

Moving stealthily between the castle and the stable, she found two large saddlebags and filled them up with the food, bedding, and borrowed clothes. Looping a rope around Sammy's neck, like she had seen the groomers do, Bianca led him out of his pen. She tossed the saddlebag across his back, tied it in place around his fat belly, and guided him toward the main gates. His little feet clip-clopped on the stones in excitement.

Then, like she had always dreamed of doing, the Frail and Delicate Princess Bianca threw open the castle gates and boldly stepped outside.

No one even noticed.

Chapter 5

Bianca had felt the sun through the castle windows, but it had never warmed her from head to toe as it did that morning. Even though it was just peeking over the horizon, she stood for a moment and basked in the yellow glow.

The student part of her made a mental note that the sun "enters in the east and nests in the west," as her tutors had taught her. From what she had overheard, the dragon and her journey lay directly in that line. She could check her way each morning by aligning herself with the sunrise.

The rest of her, the less logical and organized part, just wanted to cry with joy.

Does everyone get this thrill when the sun warms them each morning? she wondered.

Bending down, she ran her fingers through the soft grass. The sensation of it tingled up her arm. Her dream had always been to frolic through the grass and lie in the fields and stare at the sky, but that would have to wait. If someone spotted her, they would lock her up tight and never give her the chance to get away again until the flames of the dragon's breath enveloped the castle. The princess had to use great discipline and keep to her task.

The grass was temptingly green and soft, and the dust on the road kicked up under her boots and Sammy's hooves as they strode along, just as she had imagined it would. Even more distracting was the sky, massive and never-ending. The new experience was a little scary, but exhilarating at the same time. There were birds and butterflies and everything she had longed to touch and see her entire life. But she had no time for those glories now.

Finding the others, finding the dragon, was all that

mattered.

Escape from the castle was more important than frolicking.

Unfortunately, Bianca didn't really have a plan for the dragon. And she didn't have a sword. The soldiers and knights had weapons, but that didn't seem to have done any good so far. She didn't know exactly what she was going to do when she found the dragon, but she knew it was her duty to try. It was useless to just sit around the castle waiting to be attacked. On the road or in her tower, nowhere was safe with a dragon on the loose.

She might reason with him. Could a dragon speak English? Could it talk at all? She didn't have a clue about any of that beyond the fairy tales she had read. And she knew enough to understand that fairy tales were not true. Magic and spells and fairies only existed in books. She wished that were true of dragons as well.

Maybe she would find the king first. Maybe he had already dealt with the dragon and was on his way back down the road to the castle. Maybe.

Her kingdom spread out around the castle for

thousands of miles. Most of that land lay in the direction she was headed. She had done some of the math in her head. Even walking a mile or two every hour, she had a lengthy journey ahead of her.

She was grateful to have Sammy's help, that was certain. He seemed unimpressed with the load on his back and just waddled along behind her, tall ears twitching and turning at sounds she couldn't hear. She knew she wouldn't have made it very far without him.

The road was dry, and there was absolutely no traffic. From what she had overheard, anyone who lived in the direction she was traveling had cleared out a week before. Certainly, no one in his right mind was heading *toward* the dragon.

Just her.

Bianca watched for signs that her father and his army had passed that way, but rain and wind had washed away their tracks. She knew it would take her a while to reach an area where they had stopped for the night—assuming they had stopped at all.

She was going to have to be patient and observant.

The morning was less eventful than she had expected. Besides a few birds chirping in the trees here and there, she didn't encounter anything exciting or unusual. Seeing trees up close was delightful at first, but after walking past hundreds of them, she was less impressed. No people were around to question about the king and his army. Hours passed with nothing to help her on her search.

Bianca had seen a house or two on the path, but they were clearly deserted. She hadn't heard the sounds of work, voices, or animal noises, and there were no lights or smoke from chimneys. Trails led off the main road, probably to farm houses deeper in the forest. But venturing up any of them would be a waste of time. Those people had probably run to the west side of the kingdom as well.

When the sun was high in the sky, she allowed herself a brief break for some lunch. A small stream ran by the road there, and she and Sammy both enjoyed a long drink. She had never had to drink without a cup before. Watching how Sammy approached it, the princess knelt down on the shore and stuck her face right in. Sucking up that cool, fresh water felt fantastically rebellious. She imagined the look on Nanny's face, watching her dainty princess slurp up water like an animal. The thought of it made her choke a little bit and then giggle. Water ran down her chin onto the front of her shirt. She wiped it away with a sleeve and smiled.

Bianca's legs ached, and her feet had worked up some serious blisters in the borrowed boots. She'd faced that problem before with uncomfortable princess shoes. It could be dealt with after lunch. Sitting down and leaning against an obliging tree, the princess took a moment to relish in the rough bark, the crunchy leaves on the ground, and the soft grass.

As she munched on some bread and cheese swiped from the kitchen, she tossed an apple to Sammy for him to crunch. She'd seen the groomers do that with horses. But while they ate, doubt began to creep in. Birds chirped in the trees around her, as they had all morning, but otherwise, the forest was still and quiet. The reality of finding a place to sleep that night worried her. Surely they'd come across a house along the way or a barn where she could take shelter. Tales of wolves and snakes and other creeping forest creatures snuck into her mind, and she shivered at the thought.

She'd also overheard stories of even stranger creatures that the servants told around the fireplace late in the night when they thought she was tucked in and asleep. Tales of ghosts and evil spirits and witches flittered through her mind. What if some of those stories were true too?

Yes, a house would be good for shelter and security before darkness set in.

Shielding her eyes from the direct sunlight, she guessed it was probably around one o'clock. She wondered if the townsfolk were standing under her window, waiting for a greeting that would not come.

"Is there anyone left to miss me?" she asked Sammy.

He swallowed the last of his apple but didn't answer.

Bianca just smiled and tore off another chunk of bread, but it made her consider a harsh reality. Would they really miss her, or would they just get on with their lives? How much difference did a silly wave from a frail and delicate princess make anyhow? Nanny always said it was the highlight of the citizens' day. Bianca was beginning to doubt that was true.

Her uncle would surely be in a panic by now. His precious little niece had run off to become a dragon's dinner. He would imagine her collapsed along the road somewhere, too weak to fend for herself.

Bianca felt the warmth of blood rising up to her cheeks. She'd show them! She'd prove them wrong. She was not just some tiny little thing that had to be pampered and guarded. She could do something that mattered to her citizens—something of value.

Grabbing another pair of socks from her bag, she pulled off her boots and added an extra layer of protection for her sore feet before she set off again.

She would show them all.

Around midafternoon, Bianca encountered her first clue. It was a large, abandoned campsite in a clearing by the side of the road. Remnants of several campfires and torn up ground from tent stakes were clear evidence that a large group had been there.

"Oh, Sammy, they were here!" she exclaimed.

The donkey was not impressed, but he did take the chance to sit down for a break while Bianca explored.

After tying him to a tree, she scouted over the area for clues.

The soldiers and her father hadn't been traveling as fast as she had expected. Of course, when they began their journey, there were still villagers to talk to and side roads worth exploring. Bianca guessed she had caught up to the end of the first day of their expedition.

They had all survived that long. Finally, something encouraging.

The soldiers had been very tidy and respectful of the land, so there wasn't much to see. Bianca considered staying there for the night, but daylight would last for hours, and she didn't have soldiers to stand guard while she slept. Finding a house was still a better plan, so she and Sammy set off again.

The princess didn't notice the pair of green eyes watching her from the edge of the forest.

Chapter 6

As the sun began to set behind her, Bianca spotted buildings along the road. They looked as deserted as everything else had. Tying Sammy to a railing out front, she peered in the windows of the largest building. It was dark inside, but there were lots of shelves along the walls filled with boxes and bottles and other items she couldn't identify.

"This must be some kind of roadside store," she said to Sammy.

He snorted in response.

The door was locked, but there were other structures that still held some promise. Behind the shop, Bianca found a small house and an even smaller barn. With darkness closing in, getting inside a building seemed like an excellent idea. Who knew what might prowl around in the dark, including a monstrous dragon? She didn't want him to find her when she was sleeping. At the very least, she was going to need some element of surprise, not the other way around.

The house was locked as well. Bianca thought the owners may have fled the dragon, but they were sure to secure their things first. She was tempted to break a window to get inside. Her father would certainly replace it for the owner. But then she thought of the barn. Checking the main door, she found that it was unlocked and deserted, except for some hay and a bit of grain.

"Sammy, they left you some dinner," she called.

He perked his ears up at that.

Settling them both in the barn seemed the easier and kinder solution. No need to break windows just yet. She had plenty of food, and she could see a stream behind the house for fresh water. The barn walls must have kept its inhabitants safe from whatever passed by at night up until then.

She led the donkey to the creek. Once they had both drunk their fill, Bianca resolved to settle in for the night.

After securing the big sliding doors behind her with the large bolt, Bianca pulled off Sammy's packs and put the grain bucket down in front of him. She made a mental note to send some replacement grain back to the shop owner once the dragon drama was done. As the donkey munched away happily, Bianca found a brush on a nearby ledge and ran it around and around on his back, the way she had seen the grooms care for horses after a long day of riding or work.

"Well, we made it this far," she said. "Nanny never would have believed I had it in me. I hope she's not too worried."

Looking at the stalls, Bianca began to miss her massive, fluffy, pink bed just a little bit. Sleeping on hay was going to be a first. She had never slept anywhere but in her own bed. And she had certainly never gone a day without a warm bubble bath. Her hair was a tangled mess, and her clothes and body emanated an odor that reminded her of the servants after a long day. No one finding her would think she was a princess, that was for certain.

Nanny would faint away on the spot with one look at me, Bianca thought, a little ashamed at how happy that made her feel.

She tied her wild curls back with a piece of twine she found on the floor, pulled off her boots to let her tired feet rest, and then she sat down on a bench and had some dinner while Sammy finished his.

After checking the security of the doors one last time, Bianca grabbed a pitchfork and made a big pile of clean hay in the back corner. She threw the blanket and small pillow from her pack over the top.

Sammy's head was already hanging low, and his breathing was slow. Bianca wondered if she should make a bed for him too. Was he just going to stand there all night? Too sleepy to worry about it, she left Sammy to his own devices. He was a donkey. He was in a barn. He could figure it out.

She collapsed onto her hay bed and was soon asleep.

She even slept through the scratches at the door

around midnight.

Sammy heard them, instinct waking him at the first scritch. But once he realized he was safe, he dropped his head again.

Sunlight beaming through the slats of the wall woke Bianca the next morning. Sammy was already rustling around, finishing up some grain he had been too tired to eat the night before.

Yawning and stretching and pulling stray straw from her hair, the princess staggered over to the door and listened for a moment. Everything outside sounded normal. A peek at the new day brought the same sights as the one before.

As she walked down to the creek, she noticed paw prints in the dust on the ground. They circled around the barn and then headed off into the woods.

She may not have had a lot of life experience, but she had read a lot of books. It was one of the few things her protective father allowed her, so she probably had the grandest library of any princess ever. She loved books about creatures she could never touch and spent hours learning details of their quirks and behavior.

These prints were clearly some kind of animal with long, sharp toenails. They were too small to be the dragon. That was a relief, at least. A dog, maybe? There were several hunting dogs in the kennels behind the castle, but she had never been allowed near them. A dog might scratch her or get fur on her. What if she were allergic? The risk had been too great for the Frail and Delicate Princess Bianca. But that didn't mean she hadn't read books about dogs and knew what their feet looked like.

Yes, they must be dog tracks, she concluded. *Nothing to worry about.*

After cleaning up a little in the stream and getting breakfast for Sammy and herself, Bianca looped the rope around the donkey's neck again, loaded up the travel packs, and led him back out to the road. He snorted and resisted leaving the barn for a moment, but she was able to coax him along.

From the rising sun, Bianca could see that they

were not heading directly east anymore. Sticking to the main road seemed more important than staying in one direction. It was still pretty much east—where the dragon had been spotted and where her father was headed. As long as she didn't get turned around and head toward home instead, sticking to the road was her best plan.

Starting off, Bianca discovered another new sensation: aching muscles. Walking for most of the day was more activity than she normally managed in a whole month. She had never done enough of anything to end up sore before.

"Do your legs hurt, Sammy?" she asked. "Mine are killing me."

The donkey batted his long eyelashes at her and plodded along, his head bobbing in rhythm with his tiny hooves.

"No, you're probably used to this," she said. "I bet they kept you busy all the time. Me dragging you down the road is just another day of work."

Sammy snorted, which Bianca took as agreement.

Once she got moving, her muscles eased up a bit,

but worry started to creep in. Maybe she wasn't as strong and able as she'd always thought she would be if she just got the chance. Doubt nagged at her.

Turn back, it whispered to her. *You can be home by bedtime. Back in the castle in your nice, pink, soft bed. Let the men handle it. You can take a long soak in the tub with pink bubbles and not have to worry about silly dragons ever again.*

"At least until the dragon comes crashing into the castle walls and burns me out of my frilly bedroom and destroys my kingdom," she challenged herself out loud.

No. She was not turning back. She'd waited three weeks for her father and his men to handle it with no proof that they had.

Her whole life she had ached for a chance to prove that she was valuable and worthy of the devotion her subjects lavished on her. It was now or never.

Singing from up ahead interrupted her thoughts.

Who in the world is still hanging around here?

No one else was visible on the road, but she had to find the source of the song. Anyone along the way must have seen her father or the dragon or both.

"Eye of bat and toe of cow.

Mix them up, I'll show you how," the voice sang.

"Hello?" Bianca called out. "Is someone there?"

Chapter 7

"Well, hello there!" a woman's voice called from somewhere along the side of the road. "What are you doing out here all by your lonesome?"

Bianca noticed a small pathway off the main road. Leading Sammy down it, she came upon a gray-haired old woman who was hanging laundry on a thick line between two tall maple trees. Huge white sheets billowed in the morning breeze. The woman waddled around the one she was hanging, groaning as she stretched up and placed the last clip.

Bianca had watched the servants doing washing

exactly like that at home, and an odd tug pulled at her heart. Never having been away from home for a single moment of a single day, she didn't recognize being homesick when she felt it.

Air-drying the sheets was the same as at home. The old woman, however, was definitely not like anything she had ever seen. Her dark-purple dress flowed around her like a robe, brushing the ground and hiding her feet. On a dozen chains around her neck, little bottles of colorful liquid shone in the sunshine. Her gray hair was swept up in a crazy bun that looked like it would collapse every time she moved.

As fascinated as the princess was with the odd woman, she wasn't sure exactly how to start up a conversation. She didn't have much practice with ingratiating herself to strangers. People usually clamored for her attention. So she simply waited awkwardly for the woman to say something more.

"Look at you, little miss," the woman finally said, peeking around the sheets. "Where are your parents? You shouldn't be out wandering with all those stories about a dragon on the loose."

"Have you seen the dragon?" Bianca asked.

"Goodness, no," the woman said, brushing a stray hair from her eyes with the back of her hand. "I don't suppose he's gotten quite this far into the kingdom just yet."

"Aren't you afraid of him? He could be here any moment."

"Question is, aren't *you* afraid of him?" The woman leveled a judgmental gaze at her, trying to size her up. "I thought all the wee ones were long gone to the west by now."

Bianca pulled herself up tall. "I'm not a 'wee one.' I'm thirteen years old."

"Ooohhh, I see," the woman said with a laugh. "You're fairly near all grown up then. But you can't be from around here. I'd know ya."

"No, I live . . ." Bianca pondered how much to share with this stranger. "I live farther to the west."

"Well, lordy be, what are you doing coming this direction?"

"I'm looking for the dragon," she admitted.

"Looking for him, are ya? Well, that's a bit of craziness if I ever heard some."

Bianca adjusted her stance slightly, trying to appear braver and stronger and more prepared to face a dragon than she actually felt.

"I can handle myself," she said. "And I can face down the dragon, if I have to. Somebody has to do something about it. We can't all just wait to get eaten or burned out of our homes."

"Well," the woman said, "if you have plans to take on the dragon, maybe I can help you out a teeny bit."

"How?"

"Come right this way," the woman said, waving toward a cottage deeper in the woods that Bianca had not noticed before. It looked a bit creaky and sloppily put together, with moss and vines growing around the door and up the sides. "I've been preparing to protect myself, just in case, but I'm sure there's potion to spare."

"Potion?" Bianca wondered.

"Next best thing to a big sword. Sometimes even better."

The woman cackled as she waddled toward her house.

Princess Bianca hesitated. Something about the situation was eerily familiar. Nanny had read her a lot of fairy tales and folk stories when she was little, along with the favorites she still read on her own. She loved the parts about fairies and talking, helpful animals and all that, but there were bad characters in the stories as well.

An old woman alone in the forest? Not scared of a dragon? A potion?

The skin at the back of her neck prickled.

"Wait a minute," Bianca whispered. "Wait. I mean, I appreciate your offer but—"

"What's the matter, dearie?" the woman called behind her. "Haven't you ever met a witch before?"

Bianca froze where she stood.

No. The Frail and Delicate Princess Bianca, more overprotected than any child in the history of the world, had never been allowed contact with a witch before. King Dominic had made sure she didn't even know about the existence of real witches.

Nanny had said, "Witches are only in fairy tales, and those who fancy themselves witches in this kingdom are a terrible, dishonest, troublesome pile of nonsense. If you ever even see one out your window, slam it tight shut. She'll throw a nasty curse on you, just for giggles. Not that it would matter because they are not *real* witches."

Thinking back on those warnings, Bianca remembered that Nanny always got a bit shifty and nervous when discussing witches. Had she been lying? Was it just one more story she had told the princess to keep her away from the real world?

That would mean witches are real and probably dangerous.

Standing in the yard of a self-declared witch, Bianca felt her confidence slide slowly into her stolen boots. She watched the witch enter the ramshackle house.

Is this one of the would-be witches? What if this woman is a bona-fide witch?

The woman in question poked her head out the door and stared at Bianca.

"So, are you comin' or what?" she asked. "I don't have all day, you know."

What horrors could there be inside that house?

If she has a potion strong enough to protect against a dragon, what other concoctions could she have stirred up? Is there one to turn a princess into a frog, just for giggles, as Nanny said?

Pondering her options, Bianca realized that, if the witch had evil intentions, there was not much she could do about it. There was nowhere to run, and her legs were too tired and sore for much running anyhow. Facing up to the danger seemed like the brave thing to do. If she was going to be turned into an amphibian, best to get it over with quickly.

After tying Sammy up to a hitching post in the front yard, Bianca tiptoed into the house.

Chapter 8

The smell hit her before her eyes adjusted to the dim light. Cook had made some interesting meals in the castle kitchen, but the princess had never encountered odors like these before. Sweet and bitter—they were spices she didn't even have the words for—all swirled up together.

"Magical potions," Bianca whispered.

"Like I told you," the witch said. "I mixed up a batch of dragon repellent when I heard the first rumor. Never hurts to have some around, and I'd be the worst witch ever if I let myself get eaten by a dragon I knew was comin.'"

"Yes, I suppose that's true."

"I mean, what kind of fool faces a dragon without any idea of how to get out of the situation alive?"

Bianca thought she saw the witch wink at her, but she couldn't be sure.

As her eyes adjusted to the faint light inside the witch's home, Bianca noticed shelves along the walls. They were covered in dust and contained bottles of all shapes and sizes and colors. Most of them had labels on them like "eye of newt" or "frog legs" or other typical fairy tale witch ingredients. An enormous black cauldron sat in the middle of the stove, and glass jars and flasks rested alongside it. The princess could imagine the pot had often bubbled with green, gooey magic potions. In the far corner of the room, she noticed a small bed that seemed like an afterthought.

"How is it you live in the Kingdom of Pacifico and have never heard of Witch Barb?" the old woman asked. "Folks come to me from all over for love potions and get-rich tonics and make-my-crops-grow spells."

"Your name is Barb?" Bianca asked, avoiding the

direct question but also a bit confused. *Don't witches have crazy names like Broomhilda or Maleficent?*

"Well, my mother used to call me Barbie, but I'm a bit old for endearments like that these days."

She eyed Bianca, fully aware the girl hadn't really answered her question.

"What goes into a potion that can protect you from a dragon?" Bianca asked, changing the subject again.

"Ah, it's not a terribly hard one. The recipe has been around for as long as there have been dragons terrorizing kingdoms, I suppose."

Witch Barb reached for a purple bottle on the shelf. It was shiny and new, instead of dusty and laced in cobwebs like some of the others. She handed it toward Bianca. The girl looked at it, but she was hesitant to touch it.

"Do you drink it?" Bianca asked.

"No, no," the witch said. "Tastes disgusting and would give you a nasty bellyache. Wouldn't work at all that way either. It's only for external use."

"You mean like on my skin? How much should I use?"

"It depends on how close the dragon is. If he's just flying overhead, a touch behind the ears will do. If he's breathing down your neck, pour the whole bottle over your head like shampoo. It's a bit pungent, but it'll do the job right."

Witch Barb popped the cork from the purple bottle and aimed the contents at the princess, motioning for her to smell it.

Bianca didn't have to get too close. A wild array of scents attacked her nose, and she pushed the bottle away in self-defense. The witch cackled with glee as Bianca coughed and sputtered.

"What's in that?"

"Ah, that's a family secret, but dragons can't stand it. Takes you from smelling like a tasty morsel to making him run in fear." She recorked the bottle and handed it over, a strange smile on her face. "Remember, if he's close, pour it all over your head."

Bianca took the bottle, but something about the way the witch was leering at her made butterflies dance in her stomach.

What if this is a trick? What if pouring that vile

mess over my head will turn me into a cow or a troll or something worse? What if it is poison?

Nanny had said witches would do horrible things to her, just for fun. Why should she trust this one?

Bianca straightened her shoulders proudly. She was smart enough not to fall for dangerous tricks from some roadside witch.

"How do I know that this isn't just some potion that will make me shrink or turn into a beetle?"

She tried to hand the potion bottle back, but the witch just spun around and sauntered across the room.

"Why in the world would I want to do something like that to a poor little girl on a country road? That would be terribly evil of me."

"Well . . ." Bianca hesitated, not sure how to say it nicely. "Witches don't exactly have a reputation for being kindhearted. I mean, in fairy tales they are always causing trouble of one kind or another."

"Fairy tales, posh. Written by a bunch of fuddy-duddy old men to scare folks into not trusting women who live alone. I've never met a witch who would bother turning normal folks into insects and such."

Witch Barb seemed serious enough, even slightly offended. In a huff, she messed with the bottles on the shelves, as if she were looking for just the right thing. But then she spun around with a twinkle in her eye.

"Now *princesses*. That's a different matter. Witches have been known to play tricks on spoiled princesses from time to time."

Bianca's arms went goosepimply, and her scalp tingled. It was true. What Nanny had said was true. The princess didn't want to raise the witch's suspicions by running out of the house screaming, but she sure didn't want to stick around much longer either. Stepping slowly back toward the door, she fidgeted with the potion bottle.

"Oh. Okay, then. Um, thanks for the dragon potion. I'll remember how to use it if I meet up with the beast. It's probably all nonsense, anyhow. Dragons may not even be real."

Bianca had made it to the doorway. In one jump, she could reach Sammy's rope and be on her way. The witch just stood, watching her, an odd smile on her face.

"Oh, dragons are real, all right," Witch Barb said. "They really breathe fire, and they really fly through the air, and they really can gobble up young lassies on the road in one gulp. The golden ones are the worst. The nastiest. And from what I hear tell, that's what we have headin' in our direction. All bronze and golden and shimmerin' in the sun, this one is."

Despite the racing of her heart, Bianca tried to make her voice sound calm.

"I'll keep my eyes open. I can't be much for a dragon to worry about."

"Depends on what plans you have for him. Dragons can tell. Especially the golden ones. They can read your mind." The witch cackled down deep in her throat. "Little girls who really belong in pink, fluffy bedrooms have no business making evil plans against golden dragons."

Can the witch read my mind? Does she know who I am?

Maybe she just guessed about the pink, fluffy bedroom. What about the dingy-brown servant's clothes she was wearing would make the witch think Bianca had anything fluffy about her?

"Okay, so goodbye then," she said, stepping out the door and untying Sammy's rope.

"Wait a minute," Witch Barb called after her. "You are going to need something else."

She followed Bianca out with a package wrapped tightly in brown paper.

"Phew," the witch said. "It would have been terrible if you didn't have this later on. A disaster in the making."

"What is it?"

"Smoked sardines."

Bianca sniffed at the package. She couldn't smell much through the wrapping, but it did have a slightly fishy tang to it.

"I'm not sure I'll like them," she said. "I've never even tasted smoked fish before."

"Oh, don't worry. They're not for you."

Not understanding what that could possibly mean, Bianca just stood with the package in her hand. She was not sure how rude or upsetting it might be to hand it back.

"Put them in your pack already," the witch said.

Bianca figured it was easier to just comply, so she slipped the sardines into a saddlebag with the bottle of dragon potion. With a last quick smile at the witch, she led Sammy back to the main road at a quick jog.

"Thank you!" she called out without looking back.

"Don't thank me yet, Frail and Delicate Princess Bianca," the witch said. "You'd have been better off with a wolf defense potion. I never said anything about the fairy tales being wrong about big, bad wolves in the forest."

But Bianca was already too far away to hear.

Chapter 9

By lunchtime, Bianca was beginning to feel as frail and delicate as her father had always feared her to be. Her legs ached, and her feet ached, even with the extra layer of socks. All that running around in the castle had not prepared her for walking miles. Kicking up dirt in the dusty paths had grown old hours ago. It wasn't nearly as exciting as she had thought it would be.

Anxiety about her father and when the dragon might suddenly appear had frayed her nerves. Worry was definitely a new sensation. It was different than wondering about her future and who she would end up married to and whether or not she would make a good queen. She had never questioned her safety from day to day. The princess had always been secure and comfortable without anything really to fear.

But now? What if she never found her father? What if the dragon destroyed the castle and everyone in it? How many days' worth of food did she have in the saddlebags? What if the dragon found her and gobbled her up before she ran out of food, so it didn't really matter in the first place?

"I have never bothered to worry about much of anything in my whole sheltered life," she said to Sammy since there was no one else to hear. "Worry is more exhausting than all this walking."

Plopping down under a huge oak tree by the side of the road, Bianca sighed deeply.

What in the world was I thinking, setting off on this trip? Did I really believe I would find my father and his knights? What will I do if the dragon finds me first? The magic potion probably doesn't work. Even if it does, scaring him away from me doesn't help the kingdom at all.

Sammy stood next to her, his head hung low and his back leg crooked. He had already fallen asleep.

I guess a working donkey grabs his naps when he can, she thought.

Bianca wished she'd brought a horse to ride. Not that there had been any left in the stable. And not as if she knew how to ride one, but she might have figured it out. Sammy was already working hard enough, toting around food and supplies. It would be cruel to make him carry her as well. He wasn't nearly big enough for that anyhow. Her legs would nearly drag on the ground if she tried to ride him.

The princess was about to get up and find some lunch in the saddlebags, when an acorn bounced off her head. She watched it roll away in the grass and then heard laughter. It tinkled like bells, not at all like the cackles from Witch Barb. Scrambling away from the tree, she gazed up into the branches, expecting to see a small child.

What kind of child would be up in a tree on a barren road with a dragon on the loose?

A fat squirrel with a gigantic, bushy tail scurried

down the tree trunk, a nut in his mouth. Maybe he had just knocked one loose on her head. But she had heard laughter.

Do squirrels laugh? Never having met one, she wasn't sure. Her books had certainly never mentioned it.

The squirrel bounded off into the forest with adorable little leaps, but the laughter came again from among the tree branches. Bianca braced her hands against the trunk and stared up into the leaves. She saw small flecks of green and orange and blue darting around way up high, lighting on one branch and then flitting to another.

Are they insects? Laughing insects? She'd never heard of such a thing.

Bianca cupped her hands around her mouth and called up, "What are you?"

Another acorn bounced off her head, and the giggling from the tree top started again.

"Silly little girl. What do you think we are?"

"Colorful squirrels? Who can talk?" she guessed, knowing how crazy it sounded the minute the words were past her lips.

"Talking squirrels? As if!"

More laughter floated down to her.

The sparks of blue and orange and green emerged from the cover of the leaves and danced above her head. She realized that all those flecks of color were actually three distinct creatures.

"Do I look like a squirrel to you?" the blue one asked, hands on her hips in a huff.

Bianca could not believe her eyes. Each flittering creature was about the size of her hand, with translucent wings nearly as large as their human-like bodies. Not only were they vibrantly colored, but the pigment seemed to fly off and create a circle of light and sparkles in the air around them. Bianca wondered if she would get a shock if she touched one, like the static electricity trapped in her blankets on a cold winter day. Inside all of that color, the princess could see dainty little human-like faces staring at her expectantly.

She had obviously read about them in her books, but never in a million years did she think they were real.

This is just one more thing that has been hidden from me, she concluded in awe. How in the world had everyone in her life kept such a secret?

"Why, you're a fairy!" she gasped. "A little blue fairy."

"Is that so shocking?" the green one asked. "We can't be the first fairies you've ever seen."

Eyes wide, Bianca couldn't even respond.

"I don't know," the orange one whispered. "Look at her face. That's a first-time-fairy-face if I've ever seen one."

"How does a human get to be this tall without encountering a fairy somewhere along the way?" the blue one wondered. "It's preposterous."

"You are amazing," Bianca whispered, watching them flitter around in front of her.

"Goodness," the orange one said, "you'd think she had been locked away in a tower all her life, like that ridiculous princess. Hidden away from the world. So sad."

The fairies nodded at each other in agreement.

"I *am* the princess," Bianca said, not even realizing she'd said it out loud. It was as if the fairies had cast a truth-telling spell on her.

All three of them stopped their fluttering and held perfectly still, hovering in the air.

"The princess?" The green one gasped. "The Frail and Delicate Princess Bianca, who will die if she so much as sets foot outside the castle?"

"I would never have expected her to make it this far," the orange one whispered in a lilting voice.

"I know," the blue one said. "Who knew she could even walk well enough to make it out of the castle gates?"

Their hypnotic motion had stopped, and Bianca realized she was deep in the middle of it now. The fairies had heard of her. How had she never heard of them? Even the servants had avoided gossiping about them in the evenings when they didn't know she was listening. Maybe people were not supposed to talk about fairies.

And what kind of magic powers did they possess? They had already gotten her to admit to her secret without even trying. Bianca tried to come up with an excuse or a story, but the words would not leave her mouth. She tried to force out something about only being a simple peasant, but nothing came out.

"How cute," the green one said. "She's trying to make a fib. What a silly princess."

All three of them giggled again.

"You can't lie to a fairy," the blue one said. "What did they teach you up in that tower?"

"And how are you still alive?" the orange one asked. "All we have ever heard about you sounds like you can barely stand upright on your own."

That accusation rankled Bianca.

"You have been greatly misinformed," she snapped. "I am perfectly capable of walking and running and even skipping, if I am so inclined." She threw back her shoulders, feeling the need to prove them wrong. "I packed supplies, took this donkey, and I am going to find my father and his knights and the dragon. You just watch me."

The fairies hovered in front of her face. They glanced at each other in wonder. Then they looked back at her.

"Can you put on your own boots?" the blue one asked, totally serious.

"Of course I can," she huffed.

"Can you feed yourself without choking?" the orange one asked.

"Of course I can," she said, now more confused than angry.

"Were you really able to walk all this way on your own, without servants to carry you?" the green one asked.

"What in the world kind of nonsense have you heard about me? Do you really think I am so frail I can't feed myself or walk without assistance?"

The fairies looked at each other again.

The green one shrugged.

"We were never allowed to meet you," she said. "No fairies were. King Dominic ordered all fairies banned from flying within a mile of the castle when you were a baby. He was afraid the sight of us would frighten you, or we might fly into you and hurt you. Total nonsense, of course. No fairy would ever hurt a human, especially a baby. But we honored his wishes, and he never lifted the ban. So all we know about you is what we hear from the townspeople and on the wind."

Is that really what my subjects think of me? Bianca wondered.

Did they send her flowers because they loved her or because they feared she was too weak to function, maybe wouldn't survive the day? It was a sobering thought.

"My father *is* a bit over-protective of me," she said. "I was born dangerously weak, but I have grown up to be just fine. I am perfectly capable of taking care of myself."

"Does the king know you are wandering around out here looking for a dragon?" the orange one asked, her bright eyes wide. "I can't imagine that he does, or he would have turned right around and marched you back to the safety of your tower. King Dominic would let the whole kingdom go up in flames before he would let a hair on your head be singed."

That was a sweet thought, sort of. She appreciated how much her father loved her, but the image of her kingdom burning to the ground was not a cheery one. She was glad there was no way for her father to find out about her adventure. Stopping the dragon was vastly more important than saving her.

"Well, he doesn't know," she said, "and there's not much of anyone left in the castle to send after me. If they were chasing me, I'm sure they'd have caught up to me by now."

She had already considered this during her hours of walking. No one from the castle was coming to save her. It was possible her uncle hadn't even seen her note, but Nanny would have noticed she was missing at bedtime, if not before. No one was pursuing her. She was on her own.

Then she realized it was a good bet that not much got past the fairies.

"When was the last time you saw the king?" she asked.

"Hmmm," the orange one said, "must be several days ago now."

"Two weeks, at least," the blue one corrected.

"At least," echoed the green one. "He and his knights

clanked and clamored through here on their way to meet the dragon."

"But they haven't come back?" Bianca asked.

"No, my dear, they have not," the orange one said, a note of sadness in her tone. "If something horrible had happened, you'd think at least one of them would have rushed back to the castle to tell the tale. In the story books, one knight always seems to survive battles and dragons and such so he can tell the stories of tragedy and bravery."

"But this isn't a fairy story," Bianca said. "This is very real."

"Yes, dear." The blue one nodded. "It is *very* real."

"And that is why I couldn't just stay in the castle and wait for someone to fix it." Bianca gulped, tears filling her eyes without warning. "If the king is gone, I am in charge. It is my duty. It is my responsibility to find the dragon and get him to leave my kingdom alone. No one else will do it. Everyone else has run away. It's all up to me now."

She wiped at her eyes, surprised by the tears. But it felt good to let them out. It was a relief.

The fairies exchanged glances. They huddled together, their voices nothing but squeaky whispers that Bianca couldn't understand. Then they parted and faced her again.

"We will bestow a gift on you, Frail and Delicate Princess Bianca," the orange one announced.

"A gift?" she wondered. "What kind of gift can you give me?"

"Well, we have a bit of magic up our nimble little sleeves." The blue one giggled.

She flew up into the tree and returned with an acorn, which she held out in front of her proudly.

"An acorn?" Bianca asked.

She didn't want to be rude or ungrateful, but there were acorns littering the ground all around her. It wasn't exactly an exciting gift.

"Ahhh," the green one trilled, "watch."

All three fairies put their graceful hands on the top of the acorn. A low humming noise rose from them. It grew louder and louder until Bianca could feel it vibrating in her chest. Sammy lifted his head, noticing the fairies for the first time, and snorted at being woken up. His tall ears flicked and turned at the unusual sound. Just at the moment when Bianca was ready to clap her hands over her ears to block the noise, it stopped.

The blue fairy held out the acorn again.

"Take this, carefully, and put it into your pocket. Only use two fingers, now. Gently. Don't grip it in your hand. It is enchanted."

Bianca obeyed the strange orders, taking the acorn between her thumb and first finger and gingerly dropping it into the pocket of her stolen pants.

"If you are ever in grave danger—" the blue fairy said.

"You know, like if you are face-to-face with a dragon," the orange one interrupted.

"Yes, in mortal danger," the blue one continued, "all you have to do is squeeze that acorn in your fist, and it will make you invisible."

"Invisible?" Bianca asked.

"Yes," the green one said. "Even dragon magic can't make you appear."

"But take care," the orange one warned. "You won't have vanished. You will still be there and in danger, so use it wisely. A dragon could still sniff you out."

"Yes, he most certainly could," the blue one agreed.

"So make sure you can get out of his presence some other way too," the green one said. "Hide, or move slowly and carefully."

"Dragons have very good ears," the blue one whispered, as if it were a secret.

"The invisibility magic will only last for an hour," the orange one said. "So use it wisely and only when you *absolutely* need it."

"How will I know for sure that I absolutely need it?" Bianca asked.

The fairies glanced at each other and then back at the princess.

"You must wait until the only other choice is to die, I suppose," the green one said. "Save it for when you are one hundred percent out of options."

Bianca didn't want to think about that. When facing a dragon, a life or death moment was bound to happen. She'd worry about it when the time came. If she thought about it too much right then, she'd turn around and run right back to the castle. That was no good. She had to prove those rumors about her weakness and uselessness to be wrong.

She had to be brave.

"I'm sure this will protect me when I most need it," she said, trying to sound confident.

Down to the tips of her toes, Bianca hoped that was true.

"Good luck, Princess Bianca," the orange one said.

"Be brave, Princess Bianca," the green one sang.

"Persevere, Princess Bianca," the blue one trilled.

"We shower you with courage and strength and honor and blessings," they sang together, dancing in the air over her head. Sparks of color rained down on her, like magical fairy dust. "You are able to save us all, Princess Bianca!"

Spinning in a circle of color, the three tiny fairies flew off into the woods.

"Thank you!" she called after them.

With a cheering section of colorful fairies, Bianca

felt invigorated and inspired. Her feet still hurt, but her heart was bursting with pride for her kingdom. She would do everything in her power to help save them all.

"Nothing can stop me now!"

Chapter 10

Sammy had made a snack of some acorns off the ground, so Bianca grabbed an apple for herself from the saddle packs, picked up his lead, and started off down the road. Instead of listing things to worry about in her mind, the fairies had inspired her to set her thoughts on the things she could stop worrying about.

She had food enough to last a few more days. There were bound to be houses along the way that she could borrow from, if it came to that. She should stop worrying about food.

The weather was good, and there was nothing but fluffy clouds in the sky. It could be pouring rain. That would certainly have made her journey miserable, and it would wash away any evidence of her father and his soldiers. She could be grateful for the mild spring temperatures, the often-shaded roadway, and the dry path.

Her father and his knights were brave and strong and smart. She had heard about legendary battles they had fought against armies from other kingdoms who dared to invade their peaceful borders. She had to believe the king's forces were totally prepared to face a dragon. A little worry was okay, she reasoned. After all, it was her father who was in danger. She was justified in worrying about him a tiny bit, but she would really try not to.

Meeting the dragon. That was the real worry. Her pace slowed at the thought of it. She had the magic acorn now, but it would only offer limited protection. She also had the dragon repellent from Witch Barb. That could certainly come in handy, especially if she somehow teamed it up with the enchanted acorn. For a moment, she wished she had brought along a sword and some armor, but she chuckled at that image.

"Oh, Sammy," she said, "can you see me trying to fight a dragon with a sword, clunking around in a suit of armor? He might laugh himself to death at the sight of me."

The donkey tossed his head, as if he thought it would be a pretty funny scene too.

"And I bet you wouldn't have cared for lugging all of that heavy metal up and down and around this dirt road."

Sammy flicked his tall ears back and forth. No, he had no interest in that at all.

Bianca walked on, listing off the things and people in her life she was grateful for, trying to distract herself from more worries. There was Nanny, of course, who had cared for her every day of her life. Cook, who snuck her special treats when Nanny wasn't looking. Her father. A strong castle to live in. Food to eat. A helpful donkey. Strong legs to carry her down the road, no matter what others thought about how weak she was. Eyes and ears to be alert to danger.

Soon she just focused on putting one foot in front

of the other while keeping an eye on the sky. If the dragon was headed her way, and she was heading toward the dragon, they were sure to meet up in the middle eventually. It made her think of the story problems her math tutor challenged her with in her studies.

If a wagon leaves Dominic Town at 9:00 a.m., heading west at ten miles per hour, and another wagon leaves Fredericksville at the same time, heading east at eight miles per hour, what time will they meet up on the road?

If she substituted her name and the dragon for the wagons, they couldn't help but collide at some point along the road . . . assuming he was still traveling that way. She vaguely remembered how to figure out the answer, but math had never been her favorite subject.

Her tutor, Suzanna, had tried in vain to interest her in algebraic equations, though the princess did find the use of geometry in creating towering new structures fascinating. Bianca was grateful others loved math and were busy using formulas to build new inventions to make life better for everyone. It just wasn't that interesting for her.

As long as she knew enough to keep the castle running smoothly when she was queen, that was as far as her interest in numbers spread. She would much rather read a book. Then her mind could wander freely from Dominic Town to Fredericksville and every place in-between, without worrying about when anyone arrived anywhere.

Unfortunately for her immediate situation, most of what Princess Bianca loved to read were fantasy and fairy tales. Her animal books could have come in handy if she had ever studied them in any useful sort of way. She mostly just enjoyed the pictures and learning about interesting species from all over the world. The most amazing ones were from icy tundras and rainy forests where she never dreamed of going in the wildest part of her imagination.

As a child, she had made up games where she fashioned a make-believe zoo, selecting a dozen or so of her favorite creatures to inhabit her creation. Red pandas and Arctic foxes and penguins and sea lions and elephants and giraffes—animals that lived far away from her kingdom. It was her job to care for them and feed them and give them baths and brush their teeth and play with them and share what she knew about them with others. It was her own private, imaginary zoo.

Of course, she had never shared it with anyone. Not even Nanny. But being in charge of her pretend menagerie made her feel important. It was the closest she ever expected to come to animals of any kind. Pets, much less a zoo, were totally forbidden. Bianca was supposed to be far too fragile for that kind of interaction. So she had pretended and imagined.

But none of that did anything to prepare her for the real creatures that lived right under her nose in her very own kingdom. Badgers and raccoons and opossums were not terribly interesting. She'd never imagined them in her zoo. They were just forest creatures.

Donkeys were something that had never interested her very much at all either. Yet now she was spending every moment with one. He followed along on his lead and stayed with her. He carried their food and supplies. She thought she had read somewhere that donkeys could be stubborn and difficult, but she was glad Sammy wasn't like that. At least not so far. She glanced over at him, plodding along next to her, and hoped she was remembering some other animal. So far, he was behaving rather like she thought a loyal dog might.

Bianca was fascinated with dogs and always pretended to have one tagging along with her in her imaginary zoo. Wolves were slightly intriguing because they hunted in packs and were kind of like dogs. But the wolves that frolicked around in her mind were more fairy tale ones. They could talk and only seemed to be a problem if you ran into a lone, big, bad wolf.

It would have been helpful out on that lonely road through the forest if Bianca had paid more attention to what her books had to say about real flesh and blood wolves.

Back at the castle, Nanny had spent the last two days doing the jobs of seven different servants, ones who had fled and left their work undone. She helped in the kitchen, chopping and stirring as best she could. Cook seemed as annoyed with Nanny's lack of culinary knowledge as she was grateful for the help, but at least there were fewer mouths to feed. Only a dozen or so servants and guards remained, mostly because they felt safer within the castle walls than on the road. A few townsfolk had stayed close as well, camping out around the castle so they could run to safety when the dragon arrived.

Exhausted at the end of the second day, Nanny plodded up the steps to Bianca's room. She wondered if the poor girl had bothered to greet her subjects at one o'clock each day, as if it were any other old day of the week. Had anyone shown up? She also wondered if Bianca had enjoyed the meals she'd sent up to her. Nanny felt proud to actually have created a couple of those meals, and she hoped her sweet princess had liked them.

Swinging open the large wooden door of Bianca's room, Nanny was greeted by the stale odor of trays with untouched food. The lights were dim, but when she pulled the shades to reveal the evening twilight, Nanny realized the princess had not taken one bite of food from any of her meals. Six full trays of food sat untouched. Why had the servants not said anything? Did they really not even notice when they dropped off the next meal?

"The princess must be just too upset to eat," Nanny mumbled to herself.

She straightened her apron and smoothed her hair.

"Well, that changes now," she said. "Enough with all of that messing around in the kitchen and laundry room. Dragon or no dragon, I will not shirk my true duties."

The Frail and Delicate Princess Bianca was her responsibility, and she would see to it the girl got some food in her dainty tummy immediately.

"Princess Bianca?" she called out.

She checked the bathroom.

No princess.

She checked the balcony.

No princess.

She rushed to the library. Maybe Bianca had gotten bored and gone searching for a new book.

No princess.

She even checked the king's Hall of Council.

No princess.

Trying to keep her panic in check, Nanny summoned the remaining servants and demanded that they all search every inch of the castle and grounds. They raced up the stairs and down.

"Duke Frederick," Nanny gasped, rushing by him in the hallway, "did you happen to see your niece pass this way?"

"Hmmm?" he said, lifting his nose from the book he was reading. He tucked in a piece of paper to mark his place. "My niece?"

"The princess," Nanny fumed. "Bianca! Your brother's daughter!"

"No, little Bianca must be in her room. She never leaves her room."

His thought trailed off as he drifted back into his

story, no longer concerned about Nanny's presence. He slipped his bookmark onto the last page for when he would need it later.

If he had read the piece of paper he had grabbed from his desk to use as a bookmark, of course, he would have known exactly where his niece had gone. It was the note she had left him.

"Awgh!" Nanny threw up her hands in frustration.

With Bianca missing, the thought that Duke Frederick might be the only one left in charge of the kingdom haunted her as she raced down to the kitchen. She knew the child wandered the castle, even if her uncle did not.

But when she reached the kitchen, no princess.

"Oh, I should never have missed tucking her in bed last night," Nanny cried to Cook. "I was so busy helping with the laundry and the food distribution to the poor souls still inside the castle walls, and I fell asleep before I checked on her."

"Pish posh. She's around here somewhere," Cook said, stirring a huge pot of stew. "I mean, where else could she possibly be?"

Chapter 11

As the sun began to set behind her, Bianca took her long shadow as a hint that she should stop at the next house.

The afternoon had been dull and discouraging. She had started off after lunch fully inspired by the trio of fairies, but that had been the end of the excitement. Since then, Bianca hadn't seen much but trees and dirt road. The clouds floated gracefully by in the sky, but there was no sign of a dragon overhead. Wildflowers along the road were lovely, and she stopped to pick a few now and then to marvel at their color and smell.

But flowers were the one outdoorsy thing she had been allowed. They were not fascinating at all.

And she hadn't seen any evidence that her father and his knights had passed that way or made camp along the road. Maybe they had traveled faster than her. Maybe they had turned down a side road and gone somewhere else entirely.

To entertain herself, Bianca had sung some nursery songs and recited a few rhymes, trying to match her pace to the rhythm of the words.

"There was (step) an old woman (step) who lived (step) in a shoe (step)."

She had even told Sammy the stories of *Cinderella* and *Sleeping Beauty*. He appeared unimpressed and just slogged along, his head bobbing to its own internal metronome.

Bianca looped the rope over her shoulder to give her tender hands a rest from the roughness, but she was pretty sure Sammy would have followed her without a lead at that point. She wasn't, however, willing to risk it. After all, he was carrying her dinner.

There had already been several small cottages along

the path, all abandoned, so she wasn't too worried about finding another. As she had heard her father explain it, most citizens built their home along the roadway or near it—very convenient for trading or getting from here to there—then their land extended back into the forest or out to some open areas for cattle and farms. Today, all of those people were gone, but she did hear some cows mooing from back in the trees.

And she'd heard some other noises too. Leaves crunching. Twigs snapping.

Sometimes along the way, Sammy would swivel his ears or flare his nostrils, trying to snort out what was making the noise, but he never seemed to figure it out or wasn't worried about what he smelled. Bianca hoped it was the second one.

The next time the princess saw a pathway branch off into the forest, she turned down it in search of a bed for the night. Since she was looking for evidence and signs of her father, walking at night was pointless. Instinct also suggested that it was safer to be indoors. Had she just been told that for thirteen years by everyone she'd come into contact with, or was there really a good reason to have sturdy walls separating her from the forest at night? She wasn't sure, but she wasn't going to tempt fate either.

Not too far down the path, a cozy cottage lay tucked into a clearing in the trees. No smoke came from the roof, so the princess guessed no one was inside cooking dinner. She saw no washing on the line. No animals in the yard. The place seemed as deserted as every other house along the way. Well, except for Witch Barb's.

"Let's hope it's not a house belonging to another witch," she whispered to Sammy.

She knocked and got no answer. The door to the house was unlocked and swung right open. Maybe the owner was in such a rush to flee that he forgot to secure the door. Maybe he wasn't worried about someone trying to break in since a dragon was on the loose, or maybe he just didn't have anything worth stealing. Returning to find the whole darn thing burned down was probably more likely.

Tying Sammy to a nearby tree with grass for munching, Bianca looked around for some fresh water. She spotted a pump and a bucket but didn't see a stream. It could be farther into the woods, but searching for it seemed risky. The sky was getting darker by the minute. Bianca pumped a full bucket and sloshed it over near the donkey. He drank the whole thing down, so she got him another one and staggered back with it. Who knew water could be so heavy? She felt sorry for the servants who carried pails of it around the castle grounds. What an exhausting job.

Next, she checked the small barn behind the cottage. It was also unlocked and deserted, so she tucked Sammy in for the night with a big bucket of grain from a shelf nearby. After sliding off the saddlebags, she gave him a quick rinse down with another bucket of water. He shook the leftovers off like a dog, showering her with spray.

"Thanks a bunch." She laughed. "I think I'll bathe inside the house, if I can. You can have the barn all to yourself tonight."

Sammy snorted that this was just fine with him.

Picking up the saddlebags to take with her, she bolted the door to the barn so her traveling companion could get some much-deserved sleep.

As she headed across the yard to the cottage, she was greeted by a plump white cat with bright-pink ears and an even pinker nose.

"Well, hello there," she said as it rubbed against her leg. "Did you get left behind?"

Bianca had never met a real, live cat. She had pretended to have one, just like she had pretended to have all kinds of animals. Her father was sure she would be allergic to the fur, or a cat might scratch or bite her and give her a terrible disease that would kill her instantly. None of that could be tolerated for his frail and delicate daughter.

Wondering whether or not she might actually be allergic to cats, Bianca reached down and ran her fingers along the silky-soft fur. It was the most amazing thing she had ever touched. Sammy's coat was coarse and rough, but the cat felt like her fanciest velvet dress. She wanted to grab the creature up and rub her face in the fur coat, but she remembered the parts about biting and clawing and thought better of it. Best to find out if the cat was nice first.

It followed her to the front door, where Bianca now found half a dead rat of very impressive size lying on the doormat. The cat sat down next to it, blinked its eyes slowly with pride, and mewed.

"Merrow."

"Oh," Bianca said. "Thanks, I guess."

Her skin prickled a bit at the sight of the first dead animal she had ever really seen. She had a vague idea of what went on in the farmyard and in the kitchen, but she'd never seen a dead creature that wasn't prepared and part of a meal.

Bianca had read that cats enjoy giving their owners little treats like this. Maybe the gift had been meant for the owner of the cottage. Whomever the recipient was supposed to be, she was just going to step over it and leave it there. The thought of trying to move it made her shiver involuntarily from head to toe, and the hairs on her arms stood up in goosepimples. As she opened the door and took a big step inside over the rodent remains, the cat slipped between her legs and slunk in too.

"Looks like I'm going to have company for the night," she said as she closed and bolted the door behind her.

Letting her eyes adjust to the dim light inside, Bianca noticed a tidy kitchen with a large table in the middle.

The cat hopped up on the kitchen table immediately, rolled onto her back, and began to groom her privates with one back leg stuck high in the air. A female cat, Bianca noted quickly with a laugh at the total lack of dignity the animal displayed. After a scratch to the back of her white and pink ear, the cat proceeded to clean between her splayed toes with great gusto. This fascinated Bianca for a full minute before she remembered there were tasks at hand to accomplish before the sun set.

Looking around the room, the princess noticed a large bed in one corner of the cottage and sighed deeply with gratitude. A real bed was a welcome sight. More exciting than even that, there was a bathroom in the other corner with a pump and running water. Bianca had never gone so long without a bath in her life, and she had certainly never been even remotely as dirty as she was at that moment. Getting dirty required contact with dirt, at the very least, which was something that had not been allowed. The castle hallways were always a tiny bit dusty, but she had never experienced anything like the grime-covered mess she was now. After two days on the road, Bianca swore she was wearing as much dirt as she had left behind.

What faced the princess for the next hour were chores she had never expected to do in her lifetime, nor had anyone ever expected her to be capable of accomplishing them on her own. Besides being supposedly frail and delicate, she was a princess, after all. Princesses do not do laundry, prepare baths, and cook for themselves. However, Bianca was fully confident that she was up to the task of getting herself cleaned and fed and her clothes washed out. Despite knowing what to do from having seen it done hundreds of times, there was the extra challenge of being in an unfamiliar place. But she was undaunted.

"No one, including a dragon, will find me starving and bedraggled," she said to the cat, who paused for a moment to stare at her.

Princess Bianca would prove that she was perfectly capable of caring for herself.

She found two lanterns and carefully lit them both

with matches from the shelf. Then she hung them on hooks at opposite ends of the cottage.

Next, she stripped off the top layer of her clothes, down to her long underwear. After emptying her pockets and poking through the saddlebags, she tucked the dragon-repellent potion and the magic acorn in a side pocket of her boots. That would make them much handier if she needed them on the road the next day.

I wonder who thought of a clever storage spot like that?

As she pumped water over her borrowed clothes in the kitchen sink, layers of dirt and grime from the roadway ran down the drain. Adding some soap to the mix helped as well. When the water finally ran reasonably clean, she wrung them out as best she could. Then she darted outside and tossed them over the clothesline to dry overnight.

As the last light of day faded away, Bianca thought she spotted a pair of green eyes watching her from the trees. They blinked out when she stared that direction, so maybe she had just imagined it. But the snap of a twig and the rustling of leaves from that same direction made her yelp. She was certain that standing in a forest clearing in her long underwear was no way to face whatever dangers came out of the woods at night.

Running back inside, she threw the bolt and leaned against the door, catching her breath and calming her nerves. She wouldn't go back out there until morning, no matter what.

Now that the first job was done, it was time to choose next between eating and bathing. Her grumbling tummy decided the question. Sitting at the kitchen table in her long underwear, the princess had a quick dinner of bread (which was getting a bit stale now), an apple, and some travel beef jerky. It was not anything close to the type of dinners that Cook normally created for her. At home, there were gravies and sauces and herbs and spices and tender meat and fancy rices and flavorful potatoes every day. Her stomach, however, was grateful for the stale bread and the tough jerky. She could check the kitchen for something else later, but she desperately wanted to take a bath. Her scalp itched relentlessly, and there was actually dirt under her fingernails. Disgusting!

The water pump for the tub would be only cold, just like at home, but Bianca knew what she could do to remedy that. Filling a metal bucket from the kitchen sink, she hauled it over to the stove. Without maids and servants to help, one bucket of hot water was going to have to be enough.

"How cold a bath can I tolerate?" she said, glancing at the white cat, as if it might answer her.

A cold bath was not something the princess had ever contemplated. Nanny would never have let her set foot into a bathtub with water any colder than 110 degrees. Perish the thought! Bianca could die from the chill, Nanny had always fussed.

Well, there was no way she was getting the tub truly hot that night. She was far too tired to mess with heating several buckets of water. The water in the tub would just get cold while she heated the next bucket anyhow. And she was pretty sure she wouldn't die from tepid water. One bucket of warm would do.

She had seen Cook light the stove many times. The belly of this stove was already full of wood and kindling materials. Using the matches she had found on the mantle, Bianca lit the kindling and watched as the flames grew and tickled the bottom of the wood. She closed the front of the stove and slid open the venting, like she had seen Cook do.

"Fire needs air, lassie," Cook would say. "Don't want to smother it."

Wrangling the bucket of water on top of the stove, Bianca hoped for the best.

While she waited for it to warm, she pondered the whole bath situation. If she got in with her hair this dirty and washed it, she was going to be sitting in filthy, nasty water immediately. That wouldn't do. Maybe she should wash her hair separately and get the worst of the dirt out. Her itchy scalp urged her to hurry up and try it.

Finding a towel and some soap, Bianca positioned herself at the front of the tub, near the drain and the water pump. Bracing herself for the cold water, the princess bent over the tub upside down, letting her long hair flop into the basin. With her right hand, she worked the pump. It must not have been used as often as the one at the sink.

Pump . . . Nothing.

Pump . . . Nothing.

Pump . . .

On the third try, icy water from deep under the ground poured over her hair and the back of her neck.

"Aaahh!" she screamed, even though she had known what would happen.

The cat skittered off the table to hide under the bed, disturbed by the wailing princess.

Forcing herself to work the pump twice more to wet her hair well, Bianca then rubbed the soap around through her locks and the back of her neck and all over her face. It took several more pumps to rinse, and she was shivering from head to toe by the time she was done. But her scalp was much happier.

Wrapping her hair in the towel, Bianca stood in front of the stove to warm up again. Despite the frigid experience, she was very proud of herself.

"See, Nanny," she mumbled, "I won't die from a little cold water."

Warmed and recovered, she then plugged up the tub and ran the pump over and over to fill it part way. It seemed logical not to make it too deep. Then the bucket of hot water stood a better chance of doing its job.

The water in the bucket was now uncomfortably hot when she stuck her finger in, so she used pads from next to the stove to lift it off. Careful not to touch the bucket or bump against it, she poured the hot water into the tub. It wasn't anywhere near a warm bath, but at least it wasn't ice cold.

Shedding her long underwear and settling into the water, Bianca temporarily forgot about dragons and green eyes in the forest. She just scrubbed and soaked until she felt a bit more like a princess again. Running a comb through her now-clean hair helped too, though it was a massive challenge fighting the tangles without whatever lovely oils and conditioners Nanny usually provided.

Once she was cozy in clean long underwear, Bianca searched the cupboards for a more interesting dinner. It wasn't stealing, she assured herself. She would return everything she ate or used, and then some, once the whole dragon drama was resolved. There were many bags of flour and sugar and other ingredients, but she had only a vague idea how to create anything edible out of them.

Pulling more travel jerky out of her stash, Bianca chewed until she grew tired of chewing. She would have to hope for something better along the way tomorrow. She rinsed out her dirty long underwear in the sink and spread them out to dry over the bathtub edge. There was no way she was going outside in the dark. A bit more bread, some icy water from the pump, and then she collapsed on top of the bed without pulling back the covers.

As she fell asleep, the princess felt a rustling on the bed as the white cat joined her. Curling up in the small of Bianca's back, the cat began to vibrate in a most soothing way.

Purring, she thought as she drifted off. She had read about this special feline talent. It was an odd sensation that tingled along her spine.

The little white cat is so happy, she is purring.

In the clearing at the front of the house, the green eyes blinked on and off in the darkness as their owner sniffed hesitantly at the clothes drying on the line. With a snarl, he tore them to the ground.

Chapter 12

The sun pouring through the window woke Bianca early the next morning. She had not moved all night, but the cat was now sleeping in her hair. As the princess rolled over, the cat reluctantly got up, arched her back to alarming heights, stretched her front legs, and stuck her bottom in the air. Then she slipped down onto the floor. The princess had never seen anything like it.

Is she all rubber inside?

Bianca got herself fed and tidied up, grateful for a

good night's sleep indoors. The day promised to be fair, and she was sure she would find some sign of her father before that night. The closer she got to the dragon, the more confident she was that she would discover one of them.

She hoped it was her father first.

When she peeked outside before unbolting the door, Bianca couldn't see her clothes where she had left them hanging to dry. That was puzzling. It wasn't as if someone would come along in the night and steal them. That was just a silly thought. Maybe they had blown off the line. She pulled on her boots and prepared to venture out in her long underwear. Not very princess-like behavior, but desperate times called for desperate measures.

I can't take on a dragon in my underwear. Where are my clothes?

The little white cat zipped out the door between Bianca's legs, off to find her own breakfast. The princess was sad to see her go, but she certainly didn't have any use for a cat on her quest. At the moment, finding her clothes was a more pressing issue than a wandering feline.

As she stepped out the door, her foot recoiled as she remembered the bit of dead rat on the doorstep. But when she looked down, nothing was there. The hair on the back of her neck crinkled.

What happened to the rat? she wondered.

Did something else like the gift more than she did?

Shuddering, she decided not to think about that too much but was grateful again for solid walls around her while she'd slept. Another good reason to find her clothes quickly. She had no idea what creatures lived that deep in the forest and so far from the castle.

"I can just hear Nanny," she grumbled to herself as she tiptoed through the grass. "'Your Majesty has clearly lost her precious little mind.' That's what she'd say. Wandering around the forest without a weapon or any idea what might jump out and attack at any moment. Maybe I have lost my mind."

When she'd left the castle, Bianca had thought she knew enough from her books and reading to be safe. Well, except for the dragon part. But she'd never expected fairies to be real, and she'd already met them. And a witch. What else would she face that she never believed possible?

After a quick search of the yard, she discovered her still slightly damp clothes in a rumpled pile near the tree line. But worse than the disappointment of finding them still a bit wet, she discovered that something had been chewing on them. Huge sections of the fabric were torn and shredded, as if something had held onto one end and wrenched it apart. There were holes here and there as well. Holes that made a pattern of bite marks in the cloth.

In the light of a new day, Bianca's mind flashed back to the dog-like footprints around the barn the day before and the green eyes watching her from the trees. She stood up slowly and looked around. She was alone, for the moment, but she felt a bit like Little Red Riding Hood in the story books. Was this just a stray dog who had played with her clothes during the night, or was it something more? Something big and bad?

Searching for a dragon was dangerous in a fantastical, unreal sort of way. It was an adventure of epic proportions. A dragon was such a huge creature that it would be hard to miss.

But a wolf? That was a hidden danger. Wolves lurked and hunted. Wolves were a real, tangible kind of danger. Bianca felt her arms go limp, as though every ounce of strength drained out of them.

If a wolf had been following her, why hadn't it attacked them on the roadway? Surely, a donkey and a girl were not a challenge. They'd make an easy lunch. Maybe it wasn't the same wolf as the night before. Maybe the whole forest was full of wolves, just waiting to tear her to shreds like they had her clothes. She suddenly found it hard to breathe, and she strained her eyes, checking the trees around her.

Before she discovered anything, Sammy let loose with a long, frantic, angry bray from the stable. The eerie sound made her hair stand on end. The donkey hadn't made any noise more than a snort since she had met him. This racket was like that snort mixed with a squeaky wheel or a rusty door hinge.

"Haw-squee-hawwww, squee-hawwww, squee-hawww!"

He was still safe behind his bolted door, but his agitated calls made a shiver run up her spine more than the dead rat on the doorstep had. Something was very, very wrong.

Turning in that direction, Bianca saw the final proof she had been searching for. There, lapping lazily from the far side of a small creek she hadn't seen the night before, was an enormous wolf. His fur was black as coal and shone in the sunshine. Lifting his head, he stared right at her, his bright-green eyes shining. She watched his nose bob in the air as he caught the scent of her on the morning breeze.

Frozen in terror, the first genuine fear she had ever felt in her life, Bianca realized she was too far from the house to make a run for it. He could easily leap that creek and catch her before she got inside. Panic rose up, and her throat clenched as the wolf slowly splashed through the water and padded across the yard toward her.

Standing there in the clearing in her long underwear and boots, she watched the wolf growing steadily closer. Her heart beat so loud her head was throbbing, and Bianca wished she had never left her tower. What foolishness had led her face-to-face with death like this? At the moment, there was no way out. Nowhere to hide. Nowhere to run close enough to save her.

Wait, she thought. *What did the fairies say? Something about when death is the only option. A violent death at the mercy of a hungry wolf certainly seems to be my fate today.*

Time for some magic.

Keeping her eyes on the creature, she squatted down and searched the pocket of her boots. There she found the seed of magic and courage she needed to survive. Squeezing the fairies' acorn in her fist, Bianca closed her eyes and wished with all her heart that it would work.

Opening one eye, the princess noticed the wolf had stopped in his tracks. Cocking his head to one side and then the other, he whined and twitched his ears. She realized he couldn't see her.

From the wolf's point of view, his breakfast had just vanished in front of him.

Bianca sighed, but the wolf's sensitive ears picked up on it immediately. He lowered his head and growled deep in his chest. Whatever nonsense was going on, he was going to sort it out.

She took a step toward the cottage, and he lifted his

snout in the air, trying to locate her. His lips quivered with rage as his nose twitched and turned. His tall ears swiveled, trying to catch the sound of her movement. Maybe even her breath or her heartbeat. Bianca was sure he could hear that, the way it was pounding in her ears.

He knew she was there, and he would find her eventually. Hunger had shifted to frustration and anger. Magic trickery was afoot, and the wolf didn't like it one bit.

An angry wolf might be more dangerous than a hungry wolf, she thought.

Yes, she was invisible, but he could still hear and smell her. The fairies had warned her about that. But they thought she'd only be facing a dragon. Somehow that now seemed less frightening. The snarling jaws of this frustrated creature were very real and very close at that particular moment. Much scarier than a dragon she had yet to even see.

She might make it if she ran, she thought, but then she would be stuck in the cottage until help arrived or the dragon got her. That wasn't a great solution, and she certainly didn't want to sit around waiting to be rescued. She could have stayed in her castle tower for that. She was the one who was supposed to be doing the saving and the rescuing. Her father was out there somewhere. And a dragon was bearing down on the castle while she stood there in the forest messing around with a wolf.

Bianca felt courage and pride rise up in her again. The moxie that had led her to leave her sheltered castle life would have to step up and support her now. How could she face a gigantic dragon, potion or no potion, if she couldn't challenge a wolf while she was invisible?

Searching around her for options, Bianca noticed a thick tree branch on the ground, only a step or two out of reach. It was big and sturdy, but not so large she wouldn't be able to carry it. Moving slowly and keeping her eyes on the wolf, she tiptoed over and lifted the branch so she carried it across her body. She had seen the knights do that with their swords, and she had practiced using swords from the old armor on display around the castle.

She now had a weapon to defend herself. It wasn't a blade, but it would have to do. The branch didn't vanish when she picked it up, probably because she hadn't been touching it when the spell was cast.

The wolf paused and tilted his head in confusion. The branch appeared to be moving all on its own. He cocked his head again, attempting to process this strange event. A disappearing girl and a floating branch. His confusion shifted back to anger. He lowered his head, bared his teeth, and growled a low rumble.

Mustering up the courage she had felt in the hallways of the castle when she battled invisible monsters and imaginary creatures, Bianca tapped the branch slowly in her left hand.

The wolf circled around behind her, confident the girl somehow lay hidden behind the weapon.

The princess turned along with him, keeping the branch between them. Watching the muscles in the wolf's back twitch and flex, she knew the moment for real battle was upon her. He would find an opening and attack.

I'm not going to die here in the woods like a helpless child! she thought, taking a deep breath.

With a great yell, Bianca ran at the wolf, waving the branch in front of her.

"Yaaa-haaa!"

Startled, he scampered back, not sure now if he should run or fight. Encouraged by his retreat, Bianca ran forward and slammed the branch down on his bottom.

Bam!

The wolf yelped and jumped aside, hunkering down and staring at the branch.

"Naughty wolves should stay in the woods where they belong and eat rabbits and squirrels!" she yelled. "People come armed with sticks and swords! I am not breakfast, lunch, or dinner!"

With that, she swung at him again, aiming at his head this time. The wolf dodged, but he had clearly had enough of whappings from unseen humans and floating sticks. He raced off into the forest, his tail between his legs.

"And don't come back here unless you want more of the same!" she called after him.

No matter how many imaginary monsters she had

conquered in the castle hallways, she had never felt as accomplished as she did at that moment alone in the forest. It was a shame no one had been there to witness her courage because her father and Nanny would never believe it. She wished she could roar like a lion all through the woods to proclaim her victory far and wide.

Throwing back her head, she called a challenge to the sky. It came out more like the howl of a wolf, which was quite appropriate.

"Wah-hooo!"

Bianca let one end of the weapon drop and stood in the clearing. Her heart was still pounding and she gasped for breath, but she was full of pride. She—Bianca, the Frail and Delicate Princess—had scared away a wolf in the forest two days' walk from the castle.

She had saved herself.

"Bring on that dragon, and let's get this done."

Chapter 13

Once she caught her breath and her pulse returned to normal, Bianca realized that she wouldn't stay invisible for long. One hour, the fairies had said. Victory celebrations would have to wait. She needed to get dressed and get back on the road.

Returning to the house, she propped the wolf-bashing stick outside the door. It was definitely coming with her.

She was grateful she had packed an extra set of clothes. They were the same dull-brown color as the servant clothing she had worn out of the castle, certainly nothing like the fancy, frilly, pink outfits Nanny had provided for every day of her life. And they were a little big, but that didn't matter at the moment. She just needed something respectable to cover up her long underwear. Her handy suspenders had been torn to shreds, so she used some twine from the pantry as a belt to hold the pants up and left the shirt untucked. After a quick brush of her unruly hair, she tied it back again in a ponytail.

Nanny would fall over in a dead faint if she could see me now.

Then she chuckled, remembering she was still invisible. What a sight that would have been if someone had found her just then. A set of clothes tidying up the cottage all by themselves.

She left a note for the owner of the house, thanking him or her for the hospitality. *Assuming the house isn't burned down by a dragon before they return.* She frowned at the thought, but she didn't add that part to the note.

Lugging the stick and repacked saddlebags with her to the barn, she opened the doors to find Sammy waiting for her with ears tall, eyes wide, and nostrils flaring. Once he sniffed out that it was her, the donkey didn't seem terribly alarmed by her invisibility. His eyes were focused *outside* the doors. He had obviously heard, if not smelled, everything that went on during her battle with the wolf.

He stayed alert and edgy while she tied on the saddlebags and looped the rope around his neck. She was ready to go, but the donkey was not.

For the first time in their journey, Sammy refused to follow when she pulled on the rope. He wasn't even slightly interested in leaving the safety of the barn. The invisibility spell had worn off by the time she convinced him that the wolf was gone and it was safe. Finally, he let the princess lead him over to the water pump and the bucket for a drink before heading out. The donkey didn't show any interest in the small creek behind the house, and the princess was glad. The wolf was gone, for now, but another might visit that water source before long.

Bianca kept her eyes and ears open for the wolf's return, but she also knew she could trust the massive ears of the donkey. He didn't miss much, and she was confident he wouldn't let a wolf surprise them.

Securing the big stick to the saddlebags, she was ready to resume her quest.

Before they started on their journey, the white cat trotted out of the forest and right up to Sammy. He lowered his head, and the two touched noses, as if having a quiet conversation Bianca couldn't hear. With a gentle snort, Sammy tossed his head and shook his dark mane. The cat wound her way in-between his legs for a moment, rubbing all around. Then she daintily jumped up onto his back and sat down, looking expectantly at the princess.

"You can't come with us," Bianca said, hands on her hips. "We are heading toward a dangerous dragon. I can't be responsible for someone's cat."

After a slow blink of her eyes, the cat nuzzled her way into one of the travel packs with the blankets and curled up for a nap. Sammy flicked his ears but appeared otherwise unconcerned about their new traveling companion.

"Well," Bianca said, "I guess the dragon or that wolf could get you if we just left you behind. I will try to find your owners when this is all over."

With that, she looped the rope up over her shoulder. She hoped that day's journey would end with some kind of discovery—father *or* dragon. One or the other.

Neither of them could be far off now.

As the day wore on, Bianca felt the surge of courage and valor from her battle with the wolf start to ebb away. If she had the training of a soldier, she would have been warned about the crash that sometimes follows such a huge surge of adrenaline. Every valiant warrior may face this depletion of spirit after combat. But she was about as far from a soldier as anyone could possibly get. She thought the energy and inspiration to tackle evil forces would continue to drive her forward.

Instead, plodding on, step after step, she found no sign of her father, no sign of his army, and no sign of the dragon. Her heart sunk.

Maybe the dragon had already been conquered. Maybe her father had gone back to the castle another way. Maybe she was just wandering alone on a forest road being stalked by wolves. Maybe she would die out there, and no one would ever know what happened to her. It was a sobering thought.

Every noise from the forest now made her jump. Was that the wolf again? Chirping birds were no longer enchanting. Maybe the fairies would come back to encourage her and brighten up her mood.

I could sure use another magic acorn, or something even stronger.

Her feet hurt, and her legs ached, and she would even have welcomed Nanny's nagging right about then. *Lonely* was a new feeling for the princess, who had never been truly on her own a single minute of a single day of her whole pink, fluffy life. Someone had always been on the other side of every door. Now, there was no one.

And deep in her heart, she realized she was right about no one looking for her. A guard or a servant on a mission to find the escaped princess would have caught up with her easily by now. No one had missed her. No one was trying to rescue her—from her bravery or her own foolishness.

What if there was nobody left to chase her? Maybe the dragon had already arrived at the castle and burned it to the ground. She might be the only one left in the whole kingdom besides some fairies, a witch, and a bunch of wild animals.

As she thought about Nanny and Cook and her father, a sob caught in her throat and tears filled her eyes. She swiped at them as they rolled down her cheeks, but it was no use. More followed. Sniffling and wiping her nose on her sleeve, Bianca allowed hopelessness to take over. Frustration at the things she wasn't allowed to do had brought her to tears many times in her life, but this sense of utter despair was new.

"Everyone is probably dead. And the dragon will kill me too. And that will be the end of it," she moaned. "I should have stayed at home. Then I could have died with people who love me."

With one long sob, Bianca sat down right in the middle of the road. She felt like her tired legs would not carry her another step.

Sammy stopped next to her. Sensing he could take a break, he dropped his head to the ground and closed his eyes.

The princess looked over at him and sighed.

"I wish I didn't know about any of this, just like you, silly donkey. Then I could carry on with my life without any worries either."

But what were the options? She could sit in the middle of the road feeling sorry for herself and crying and wait for someone to come save her—or something to come kill her—or she could get up and continue on. In the end, those were her choices.

Wiping her tears with her sleeve again, Bianca got back to her feet and dusted off her pants.

"Enough pity party. Forward we go."

As soon as she spoke, Sammy's head came back up, and he waddled along again. She scuffed her boots in the dust of the road, raising up little clouds around her feet. Sammy snorted as the powdered earth swirled up into his face.

"Sorry, Sammy," she said, waving a hand in front of him to clear it.

Hearing all the fuss, the little white cat poked her head out of the saddlebag.

"Well, hello there," Bianca said. "Did you have a nice nap while we slogged along the road?"

The cat gracefully crept out of her hiding place and stood in the middle of Sammy's back on the strap that held the saddlebags across him. Swaying with the rhythm of the donkey's walk, she stretched and drug her claws violently through the leather strap. Then she sat down and began a session of detailed licking and grooming.

Bianca smiled and wiped the last of the tears from her eyes. The ridiculous sight of a cat taking a bath while riding on a donkey overcame her melancholy. A laugh broke through the lump in her throat, and she shook her head to clear her thoughts. Crying was a waste of time and energy.

She was still the princess. Nothing about her mission had changed. She still had a duty to her kingdom or what was left of it. She had to persevere.

"It's not like I have a lot of options at this point anyhow," she said to Sammy.

Bianca turned to walk backward and watch the cat's contortions, fascinated by the bathing process. Again, she wondered if the creature was lacking some bones.

"How can you bend like that?" she asked.

The cat froze, mid-lick, her tongue still hanging out of her mouth and her back leg in the air with her toes splayed. At first, the princess thought the creature might respond to the question, but then she noticed that Sammy's ears were twitching and turning. Both of her animal friends had heard something.

Stopping in her path, Bianca listened too. Without all her clomping and sniffling, she could hear what sounded sort of like water gushing out of a pump or being poured into a bathtub. It wasn't anything she had ever heard in her life.

Sammy flared his nostrils and lifted his head eagerly. Following his lead, the princess sniffed the air too. It was fresher and clearer than normal, but she couldn't quite place why.

Without waiting for her, Sammy started walking again. His little feet clip-clopped as fast as they could go without running, his head bobbing wildly and ears alert. The cat stood up tall and gripped her claws into the leather strap. Bianca had to trot to keep up. She couldn't take a chance at losing the donkey, and he was intent on heading toward the sound.

One thing she had learned that morning: it was useless to argue with a determined donkey.

Before long, the source of the excitement came into view. A wide river lay across the road ahead of them.

Chapter 14

Once he caught sight of the river, Sammy sped up his trot until the princess had to flat-out run to keep up. The cat jumped free of the rattling ride and strolled up to the water's edge. Leaning over the grassy bank, Sammy and the cat both enjoyed long drinks from the quiet water that lapped gently at the shoreline. Bianca just stood with her hands on her hips, trying to catch her breath and pondering the situation.

Remembering her geography lessons, Bianca realized that she was standing on the banks of the river named after her mother: Ariana's Waterway. She burst into tears again at the thought of the beautiful queen she only knew from paintings and stories. Ariana the Kind. Ariana the Just. Ariana, the queen who had died giving birth to Bianca. She hoped her mother would be proud of the journey she was on and her quest to save the kingdom. In her heart, she believed she would.

Wiping her eyes, Bianca faced the problem at hand. There was no bridge. That seemed odd on a main road, but it was the fact of the situation.

Something I'll have to remedy if this dragon nonsense is ever over, she thought.

Assessing the size of the challenge, Bianca figured it would take her about five minutes to walk across the waterway if there had been a bridge. She could see the other side, but it was a long way off. Building a bridge would have been an enormous challenge. Probably why there wasn't one. It would require lots of geometry. Of that she was certain.

On the far side of the river, she saw a large raft. It was connected to a rope that ran across the span of water and was tied to a tree on each side. She had heard of things like that. Someone would pull you across the river on the raft, and it was connected to the rope to keep it from washing away in the current. The raft itself looked large enough to hold a wagon or two and several horses, so it probably worked well in the country. It was a simple and effective way to cross. But there was one major problem. The raft was on the far side of the river from the princess, and she saw no one over there to bring it back. If there was a way to retrieve it on her own, she didn't know how.

The presence of a raft like that also meant that the water was too deep to just slosh across. She couldn't remember any exact depth and width numbers on the river from her school lessons, but if a raft was required, it was clearly too deep for her to manage on her own.

Bianca squatted on the riverbank, scooped up some handfuls of water, and slurped them down. Then she sat on the grassy hill behind Sammy, still holding his lead.

Once he finished drinking, the donkey sat down on the shore, drooped his head, and closed his eyes. The cat climbed up on the hill next to them and began washing her furry face with a front paw.

"So, is this the end of the line?" Bianca asked the cat, as if she would answer.

The cat paused her cleaning and stared intently at the princess. Bianca noticed for the first time that the creature had one green eye and one blue eye.

"Fascinating," she said, leaning in closer for a better view.

In response, the cat tipped her head up and bumped noses with the princess. Then she resumed her grooming.

Bianca was so shocked that she froze. Then she reached up and touched her nose where it was still a bit cold and wet. She'd never had an animal do something friendly like that. There had always been a fence in the way, and her father would certainly never have allowed her to touch noses with the dogs in the kennels. She smiled and reached over to pet the cat's soft white head. The cat purred and stretched out in the warm grass, allowing the princess to rub her furry belly. It was softer than anything Bianca had ever felt in her life.

“I suppose you have a name of some sort. I’m not sure what people call cats. How about Miss Kitty? Will that do for now?”

Miss Kitty just rolled over in the grass, totally content, so the princess took that as a yes.

Looking upstream and downstream, Bianca noticed side roads that led away along the riverbank, off into the forest. There were all kinds of human and horseshoe prints, but she had no way to tell who had made them. Had her father and his knights gotten stuck there too and headed in one of those directions? The sun was high in the sky, so she decided to take a quick lunch break and consider what her next steps should be.

North or south? Go back?

Sammy didn’t open his eyes when she reached inside the saddlebag, but one of his ears swiveled in her direction.

“Just grabbing some food,” she whispered.

His ear twisted back to the front again, and he sighed.

Bianca pulled out dried fruit and now very crusty

bread. Remembering the package of smoked sardines the witch had given her, she pulled them out as well. But the little fishes didn't smell appealing to the princess at all. Maybe if she got really super hungry. What had Witch Barb meant when she'd said that Bianca would need them? Was she supposed to save them for when she was dying of hunger, like the acorn was just for when death was the only option? No. The witch had said that they weren't for Bianca at all.

She glanced at the little white cat.

Cats eat fish, don't they?

The princess opened the wrapper and offered them to Miss Kitty.

At the smell of the fish, the cat raised her head immediately, delicately pulled one sardine out with her tiny front teeth, and dropped it in the grass. After a thorough sniffing and a hesitant lick, she gobbled it down and went back for another.

The sardines were never for me, Bianca thought. *Did Witch Barb know I would meet up with a cat? With this specific cat?* If she ever saw the witch again, that would be one of her first questions.

She broke apart the loaf of bread that was nearly stale. There were some veggies left as well, but she was getting down to the end of the fresh food.

Maybe going back to the cottage was the best choice. She saw no visible way to cross the river. The food she had packed wasn't staying as edible as she had hoped it would. As it turned out, bread was not very hardy. Her morning adventures with the wolf crossed her mind, and she realized there were certain to be more creatures in the woods she would have to tangle with if they didn't find a safe place to spend the night. She stood and checked up and down the shoreline again, hoping for an answer.

"What do you think, Miss Kitty?" she asked. "Should we go back to your house? There's no way to cross this river. You and Sammy could probably swim it, but I can't. I never learned how. That's not surprising, I'm sure. I never learned how to do anything really useful. You may have heard that about me. Sammy might be able to pull me across, but that current looks pretty fast in the middle. If I lost my grip . . ."

Miss Kitty glanced up at her with big mismatched eyes and blinked slowly. Her whiskers were wet from the sardines, but she looked totally content.

Bianca laughed at herself.

"I'm talking to a cat," she mumbled, tossing the stale end of the bread loaf into the water where it could be food for something less picky.

"Meerrrow," Miss Kitty trilled back.

"Do you have a solution for me?" Bianca asked. "Do you have some magical way to get that raft over to this side of the river? I could really use some magic right about now."

Without hesitation, Miss Kitty licked the sides of her face to clean her whiskers and then focused across the river at the raft. She tipped her head, as if considering the situation. Then she stood up, rubbed along the side of Bianca's leg, and sauntered to the edge of the water, her tail held high in the air. Turning to glance back at the princess, Miss Kitty trilled again.

"Meerrrow."

"Are you going to swim across without me?" Bianca asked. "Be careful. Do cats even swim?"

But Miss Kitty didn't step into the water. Instead, her fur puffed up, and she shook herself gently. Then, from the middle of her back, two delicate, pink, gauzy wings unfolded. The cat flapped them gently, and they sparkled in the afternoon sun. She looked like a teeny-tiny, furry version of the mystical flying horse Pegasus that the princess had read about.

"Wow," Bianca whispered, scared to move or say much more.

Miss Kitty is clearly not an ordinary house cat.

After testing her wings for a moment, Miss Kitty flittered into the air. She moved more like the fairies, not all flappy like a bird. The dainty fairy cat hovered for a second with her legs hanging below her, then glided out over the water and across to the raft.

Bianca shielded her eyes from the sun and watched across the water as Miss Kitty landed on the rope and the upright bar that attached it to the raft.

Digging in with her claws, the cat fluttered her wings and slowly pulled the raft back toward the shore where Bianca waited, open-mouthed. Once the raft was docked and secure, Miss Kitty landed back on the shore, shook herself again, and the pink wings vanished.

"Meerrrow," she announced with authority.

"Thank you," the princess said, sitting down hard on the bank behind her.

Miss Kitty then groomed her fur back into place, clearly satisfied with a job well done.

"Okay," Bianca said. "I guess it's across the river we go."

Chapter 15

Bianca repacked the rest of her lunch items and picked up Sammy's lead to start on their journey across the river. The donkey hadn't opened his eyes during Miss Kitty's aerial display, but when he felt the princess reach for the rope, he snorted and rose to his feet.

The princess walked up next to the donkey and put her hand under his chin, staring into his big, brown eyes.

"Do you have any special magical powers I should

know about?"

Sammy batted his long, thick eyelashes. If he had secrets, he didn't share them.

"Come on, Miss Kitty," Bianca called out. "Time to cross."

The little white cat looked up at her, but she didn't move.

"I guess I really don't need to be worried about you after all," the princess admitted. "I thought I was going to be responsible for protecting you and keeping you safe, but I'm betting you can take care of yourself just fine."

Miss Kitty blinked—slowly and deliberately—and then yawned and wiped a paw across her nose.

"Let's go about this a different way. Sammy and I would love to have you come with us. Will you join us in crossing the river, or are you going to head back to your house?"

The cat hesitated for a moment, gazed down the road, then rose and trotted over to the donkey. Hopping back up on the saddlebag strap, she settled in for the ride on the raft.

"Hang on," Bianca said. "I'm not sure how Sammy is going to feel about stepping out onto this raft. It all has me a bit spooked, but maybe he has done it before."

The raft seemed secure enough, but it bobbed up and down in the waves at the shoreline. Falling in the water at this point wouldn't be a problem, but what about once they had worked their way out into the middle where the current was whooshing along? Bianca took a deep breath and prepared to step out onto the wide, wooden surface.

Sammy was happy to follow to the river's edge, but he made it absolutely clear that he was not stepping onto the floating raft. No way. No how. He had not done it before, and he was not doing it now. Common sense told him that the ground should be solid. To him, the raft looked unstable as it moved up and down. The donkey sat his rump on the beach and would have none of it.

Hoping to reassure him, Miss Kitty hopped onto the raft.

She walked around on the flat surface.

She rolled on her back to show him how safe it was.

Sammy was not impressed. He snorted and laid his ears back.

Bianca used her full weight to pull on the rope around Sammy's neck, hoping to just drag him onto the raft. No luck. He just stretched out his neck and dug in his hooves.

She got behind him and tried to push him forward with her hands, her shoulders, and even tried using her bottom to gain some leverage against his back. Her feet just slid out from under her, and she landed with a thud back to back with him. The donkey didn't shift an inch, but he flared his nostrils and held his ground.

Try as she may, no amount of pulling or pushing would budge him. He had decided the raft wasn't safe, and that was the end of it for him.

"Well, this is silly," Bianca said, standing up and putting her hands on her hips.

She wiped sweat from her forehead and retied her wild, curly hair out of her face. The donkey had been a big help so far. She couldn't face what was on the other side of the river without him. Yes, he carried her food and supplies, but just his quiet presence had become a great support. Her face flushed as the heat of frustration rose up in her cheeks.

"Miss Kitty sprouted wings to get this raft across the river for us, and you won't get on? That's just downright annoying. We haven't found anything on this side of the river. My father could well be the person who left the raft on the far side when he and his men crossed. You need to get your stubborn donkey hind end up and onto that raft. Now!"

Sammy glared at her, the whites of his eyes showing, and laid his ears back even farther.

"Do you know who I am?" the princess asked.

Sammy grunted.

"I guess it really doesn't matter to a donkey if I'm a princess or not. Or maybe you've just heard stories about how frail and delicate I am. But I'll tell you what. I'm the frail and delicate princess who scared a wolf off into the forest just this very morning, and I'm not going to be stopped by a cranky donkey."

It had been a long time since Bianca had found

herself in the middle of a full-blown temper tantrum. As a child, they were a frequent event. Nanny and her father wouldn't let her do anything fun and exciting, and she had often flopped onto the floor in a screaming rage. But fairly early on she realized that would get her nowhere. The grown-ups were not going to yield. She had learned to accept her lot in life. But while facing off against the stubborn donkey, the princess felt her anger rise as it had when she was two years old.

"Stupid donkey!" she yelled. "You are getting on that raft and crossing that river!"

Sammy, for his part, was as unmoved and undaunted as Nanny and the king had once been.

As Miss Kitty watched, Bianca pushed and pulled and shoved some more, but Sammy remained solid as a rock on the river's edge.

Sweaty and hot and furious, Bianca yanked the big stick from the saddlebags. It had worked with the wolf that morning, and it should work with the donkey too.

"There's more than one way to make you move!"

she yelled, waving the stick in front of his face.

Sammy cocked his head sideways and glared at her. It was not the first stick he had run across in his life. He understood the threat, but he was still not getting on that raft.

Bianca stood, stick in hand and ready to swing, glowering at him.

Sammy just glowered right back.

In the middle of the standoff, Miss Kitty trotted over and wiggled her way into one of the saddlebags. Bianca was determined not to be distracted by the cat, but then Miss Kitty backed out of the bag pulling a huge carrot by its green, leafy top. The white cat dragged the veggie over and dropped it at the princess's feet.

Looking down at the cat's gift—much nicer than the dead rat the day before—Bianca noticed that Sammy was eyeing it as well. His nostrils flared, giving it a good sniff.

"Oh, you like that, do you?" she said, picking up the carrot.

She held it out toward him, and Sammy stretched his neck as far as it could go without getting up. He reached with his lips, smacking in the air.

"Carrots are yummy and delicious." Bianca tempted him, running it along under her nose and taking a bite off the pointed end.

"Haw," Sammy bellowed, his big teeth flashing in frustration. "Haw squee-haw squee-haw!"

"Well, come get some then," Bianca said, holding it out again and tucking the stick under her arm.

Sammy stood up and stepped one foot forward, just able to reach the green stalk and take a couple of nibbles. As Bianca walked backward, Sammy followed, a step at a time, grabbing bits of green and then chomping on the delicious orange treat with glee. He was so focused on the carrot that he didn't notice where the princess had led him. By the time he was done chewing, Bianca had already started pulling on the rope, carrying all of them away from the shore before he could change his mind.

Balancing himself in a panic, Sammy realized too late that he was on the raft and floating. He froze in place, legs spread wide and straight, sensing it was better to be still on that uncertain surface than to try to escape in the flowing water. Miss Kitty had sprouted her gauzy, pink wings again and fluttered around above his head.

For a donkey who had spent his whole life working at the castle, it had become the oddest day ever.

Bianca wasn't any more comfortable on the raft than the donkey. She was careful to keep both hands on the rope as much as possible as she pulled them across. In the middle of the river, the raft swayed from side to side. Small waves lapped up along the edge of the wooden surface. She focused on the far shore and did her best to stay calm. If she and Sammy both panicked, they might both fall in. She didn't dare look at the water flowing past them and splashing up around her feet.

Once the raft bumped and settled onto the far side of the riverbank, Sammy leapt off at once. When his hooves hit the grassy bank, he sat down, making it clear he was not getting back on. Bianca stepped off the raft and walked over to him, feeling the same way herself.

"It's okay, Sammy. It's over now. Let's both hope we don't have to do that again."

She pulled another carrot out of the bag and fed it to him, rubbing the hair patch between his ears.

"I'm glad I didn't hit you with the stick," she admitted as she tied it back onto the saddlebag. "It probably wouldn't have helped, and I would have felt really bad in the end. Miss Kitty had a better idea."

The donkey munched away, not really clear about exactly what had happened but glad it was over.

Searching around the mud and sand on the shoreline, the princess saw footprints from horses and people, but it was impossible to tell if it was her father and his soldiers or just farmers and country folks fleeing the dragon. The trails went up and down the shore, as well as off along the thoroughfare ahead into the forest.

She sighed and turned toward the dirt road. More trees. More miles to travel.

Miss Kitty landed on the grass nearby. Her wings seemed to dissolve into thin air. Then she rolled and stretched and flopped there in the sun.

"I agree," Bianca said. "Let's take a break before we continue on. That was exhausting."

Collapsing on the grass between them, the princess kept a light hold on the donkey's lead as she gazed up into the vast sky. But she didn't need to worry about him getting away. Sammy was already asleep, sitting right where he was.

As Bianca watched the clouds float by, as she had many days from her bedroom window, she worried about her father and the castle and the dragon.

What if it is already too late?

Chapter 16

Back at the castle, Nanny sat at the kitchen table. Tears rolled down her cheeks. There had not been a single sign of her beloved princess, and she didn't know where else to look.

Cook patted her distraught friend on the back gently and placed a bowl of stew on the table in front of her.

"Eat, Nanny," she coaxed. "Have some lunch, then we will go check the stable and kennels again. You know she always wanted to go there. Maybe she just fell asleep out with the puppies or something."

Nanny shook her head. They had already checked those areas twice.

Bianca was not playing with some puppies.

She was gone.

As Nanny poked at her stew, Duke Frederick meandered into the kitchen, looking for some lunch. Normally, a maid would bring food to his room, but no one had time for those pleasantries. He lifted his eyes from the book he was reading long enough to find a seat at the table and nod politely to Nanny.

Cook slid a bowl of stew in front of him and plopped a fresh loaf of bread on the table on a cutting board that sat between them. When Nanny and the duke both ignored it, Cook sighed and began cutting off some slices.

"I suppose you'll just keep reading until the dragon arrives," Cook mumbled.

"What's that?" Duke Frederick said, lifting his eyes to meet hers.

"Nothing, Your Grace," she said, returning to the stove but grumbling the whole way.

Preparing to eat, the duke set his book on the table

for a moment while he put his napkin on his lap and found his spoon. He marked the page carefully with the piece of paper he had been using the last few days. As he picked the book up again to read while he ate, the paper slipped out and slid across the table, landing in front of Nanny. Absentmindedly, she grabbed it to return it to him, but the handwriting on the paper caught her eye.

A moment later, an unearthly wail of grief shattered the quiet kitchen. It echoed through the hallways, through the throne room, the Hall of Council, and out into the empty courtyards of the castle.

Cook nearly spilled the whole pot of stew.

Frederick froze, spoon halfway to his mouth, and lowered his book to stare at Nanny.

As for Nanny, her cry of horror finally stopped, and she clutched the paper to her chest.

"Whatever in the world is wrong?" Cook said, waddling over.

"Did you read this paper?" Nanny glared at Frederick.

He glanced at her over the top of his book and then

looked at it.

"Why would I read my bookmark?" he asked.

"You read everything else!" Nanny yelled and banged her fist on the table.

Cook and Frederick both jumped, and the duke set his book down next to him. Nanny had never behaved so irrationally.

"It's a note from Princess Bianca," Nanny said.

"Ah, from my niece," Frederick said, as if having that information solved everything.

"Yes, from your niece, who we have been searching for everywhere."

"Well, what does it say?" Cook wanted to know.

"She says . . ." Nanny gasped and clutched the paper tighter. "She says that she has gone off to find her father and stop the dragon on her own."

The bubbling of the stew was the only sound for a solid minute.

"She went looking for the king?" Frederick finally asked.

"Yes," Nanny said, nodding her head slowly.

“And the dragon?” Cook asked.

“Yes.”

Nanny laid her head down on top of her arms on the table. Every bit of energy drained out of her. Her charge. Her princess. Her one duty and responsibility in the world for thirteen years was gone.

“She left the castle?” Cook sat down next to Nanny, still holding the spoon from the stew.

“Yes,” Nanny said. “Our little princess has been alone in the woods for nearly three days now. Two whole nights. You know what that means?”

Cook and Frederick stared at her, waiting for her conclusion.

“It can only mean one thing.”

Nanny raised her head, straightened her dress, smoothed her hair, and placed the crinkled paper on the table in front of her in sad resignation.

“Our Frail and Delicate Princess Bianca is dead.”

Chapter 17

Unaware of the hopelessness unfolding back at the castle, Bianca slogged farther down the country road. The futility of her journey was beginning to wear on her again. Her shoulders slouched and her boots dragged in the dirt, but the princess went on, step after step.

Miss Kitty trotted along behind her, but she often ventured off into the trees and out of sight. Bianca left her to her own devices. A fairy cat, or whatever she was, could certainly take care of herself.

The princess had been positive she would find some sign of the soldiers and her father on the far side of the river. But still, there was nothing. It was growing harder and harder to stay optimistic and focused.

"Everyone could be dead," she mumbled to herself, "and I'm just traipsing through the forest like a fool."

Then, without warning, Sammy began braying. His lips flapped, and his white teeth gleamed as he pulled against the rope Bianca had led him by for days.

"Haw squee-haw squee-haaawww!"

"Sammy, what on earth is wrong?" she asked, trying to calm him down.

Holding tighter to the rope, the princess checked around for any sign of the wolf or other danger, but she couldn't find anything wrong.

The donkey's giant ears spun and twitched, the whites of his eyes flashed, and his nose wiggled around like a bee had gotten stuck inside. No, he was not staying there! With one giant tug and stretch of his neck, the donkey yanked the rope over the top of his head and was free. Then he turned and galloped back down the road, far away from the terrifying menace he could both hear and smell.

Bianca stared after the escaping donkey, the rope limp in her hand.

“Sammy! No! Wait!” she called, knowing that chasing him would get her nowhere. He could easily outrun her and showed no signs of slowing down. She watched him run flat out, something she didn’t even know he could do. Eventually, he rounded a bend and was out of sight.

“What spooked him like that?” she wondered aloud.

Not even the wolf had that effect on the donkey. She searched nervously all around her, but she couldn’t see anything.

Maybe he has the right idea, she thought. *Maybe it’s time to turn around and head back home.*

What was left of her food had galloped off down the road with the frightened donkey, along with her big stick for beating away wolves. Sammy would stop when he got to Ariana’s Waterway. She might meet up with him there, unless he wandered off down one of the side trails and into the woods.

As she pondered what to do, a gentle breeze blew past her, and she noticed a strange odor. It was unlike anything she'd ever experienced. Granted, she hadn't been exposed to a lot, but this smell was totally peculiar.

Rotten eggs. Eggs found months after an Easter egg hunt was the closest thing she could relate it to.

That had happened once in the castle. Nanny had hidden a few eggs so well that Bianca hadn't found them until the harvest celebrations later that fall. She had accidentally dropped one, and it had splattered on the stone floor with a stench she would never forget. That same nasty rotten-egg smell wafted past her again.

Where was it coming from? Was there a chicken farm nearby?

Walking into the edge of the forest, Bianca also noticed a wheezing noise. It sounded like Nanny snoring after she'd had one too many pints of ale with the servants, but it was ten times as loud as Nanny on her worst night.

Bianca was tempted to run away, but what if it were

the soldiers resting just off the roadway? Steeling her nerves, Bianca continued forward, but she walked slowly and carefully, like the wild natives she had read about in books.

Quiet. Quiet.

As she peeked through the trees, she spotted a large clearing up ahead in the forest. The noise and the smell were coming from that same direction, so she crept toward it. Parting the branches of some bushes at the edge of the clearing, Bianca stifled a gasp.

There it was.

After all that time.

Right there.

The mighty dragon himself was snoozing in a large field of clover, oblivious to the tiny princess. His deep-bronze and gold scales sparkled brightly in the afternoon sunlight. His solid, wide body was sitting upright, and his long neck curled around so his head was tucked neatly under one wing.

Bianca's skin prickled. She had read about dragons in her fairy tale books, but seeing one in person was breathtaking. He was quite simply enormous. She had always been impressed with the working horses in the kingdom with their massive muscled backs and clomping hooves, but the dragon put them all to shame.

The princess crept into a patch of bushes a short distance away and watched the dragon sleeping.

He seems quite peaceful, she pondered, listening to his rhythmic snores.

Yet, just at that moment, the dragon gave a snort and a shake and unfurled his colossal wings for a drowsy stretch.

Bianca watched in awe as the golden wings reached higher and higher and farther and farther until they blocked her view of the sun.

He could hug my tower in the castle with those things, she thought.

Of course, she realized that a hug was probably not what it would feel like. She shuddered but didn't take her gaze off the dragon.

With his wings out of the way, she noticed he had four legs and taloned claws. His head was massive, with a long snout like a dog, and two small horns jutted out of the top of his head above his ears. His eyes fascinated her—all glinty and green and multifaceted, like a skillfully cut diamond.

His long neck reached up high, and a small puff of fire spouted from his mouth. With the rays of the sun pouring down on him all golden and shimmery, the dragon was truly a glorious sight. In her amazement, the princess forgot to be quiet and forgot to be afraid and simply gasped "Ooohhh!"

Bianca immediately clapped a hand over her mouth, but it was too late.

The dragon stopped mid-stretch and swooped his head down to where the princess was hidden. Tipping his head, one of his emerald eyes scanned the tree line for the human he knew must be there. He took a deep sniff. Then he grinned, his emerald eyes glowing.

"Who is spying on me this afternoon?" he rumbled.

Much to the princess's surprise, the dragon pushed his nose right into the bushes where she was hiding. He sniffed and snuffled, working his way through the undergrowth, until the tip of his snout was just inches from her face. The princess was surrounded by the dragon's steamy, rotten-eggy-smelling breath.

In the back of her mind, Bianca knew she should be scared. She should have been *terrified.* That was the logical response a frail and delicate princess could reasonably be expected to have when she found herself alone in the forest and face-to-face with a monster. But instead of being frightened, the princess was filled with fury.

She imagined her father and his knights bravely fighting this creature—but being slaughtered instead of victorious. She envisioned her castle and her kingdom in rubble and ruin. He might already have been there and destroyed it all. Everything she loved and everyone she cherished were probably already gone. And it was all this monster's fault. She considered the witch's dragon repellent potion that was still in her boot pocket, but she no longer wanted to escape or make him fly off to another part of the kingdom.

It was time to deal with the dragon, once and for all.

Dropping Sammy's rope, she leaped from her hiding place and stood in plain view.

"Well, what have we here?" he said, his thick, armored tail slowly swishing through the grass behind him and then curling around his feet like a giant golden boa constrictor.

"I am Princess Bianca, ruler of this Kingdom of Pacifico that you are lumbering through. I've come to tell you to get out. Now!"

The dragon tilted his head up and laughed so loudly the ground and trees around them quivered like an earthquake. The princess had trouble keeping her footing until he stopped and stared down at her.

"Are you, a puny little peasant girl pretending to be a princess, ordering me around?"

His thunderous laugh echoed through the forest again, but this time it was tinged with a rumble and a growl and a threatening sound that silenced all other noise in the woods.

Lifting his head to its full, dizzying height, the dragon bellowed a challenge to the kingdom. Flames leapt from the dragon's golden jaws, blazing through the sky above the forest.

Princess Bianca didn't flinch. Her tiny feet slipped

around inside the stolen boots, but she planted them firmly on the mossy ground and stared straight up past the bronze, armored belly of the beast that threatened her kingdom and every living being for miles around. There was nowhere to run. There was no way to fight. But she was going to do what she came there to do.

As the last flames blew away in the breeze, the dragon glared down at her, smoke billowing from his nostrils with every breath. People usually ran in fear at the very sight of him, but not this tiny girl.

"Where is my father? Where is the king? Where are the knights who rode with him?" she demanded.

The dragon bent his mammoth head down until he hovered only inches above her. Wisps of smoke swirled around her brunette curls as he chortled with amusement.

"I would imagine the same thing happened to them as every other knight and king who rides against me."

He poofed a quick flame above her head as an example and tipped his face so they were now eye to eye.

"Then you are going to be one sorry dragon."

"Is that so?" he murmured.

Chapter 18

With his jaws just inches from her face, Bianca could smell the charred odor of his breath and the vile, rotting stench from what must be nasty bits stuck in the monster's enormous teeth. It was more than she could stand. She imagined her father bravely fighting this arrogant beast and being caught up in those terrible jaws.

Did the dragon laugh before he ate him?

Has the brute already blown my kingdom to ash?

He's downright awful and disgusting and a cold-

blooded killer. That's what he is.

Bianca imagined her castle tower crumbling down into the flames that had taken away everything good and wonderful in her life. Had he burned up Cook and Nanny? Were the children who came to visit her each day running for their lives, their homes destroyed too? Or worse?

The dragon snorted hot smoke in her face again and tipped his head to the other side, wondering what she was thinking and why she hadn't run. Silly girl. He could snap her up in one bite. Was she frozen with terror?

The blood rose up hot on Bianca's cheeks, and she clenched her hands into livid fists. No. She was not afraid. Terror was the furthest thing from her mind. She wasn't scared. She was furious! In that blinding rage, the Frail and Delicate Princess Bianca raised both of her arms above her head and slammed her fists down on the dragon's nose with all her strength.

The dragon blinked his green eyes but didn't withdraw, as if confused by the sensation. So the princess slammed her fists down again, and then again. She finally had her chance to *do* something, after all those years of nothing. This monster might eat her up in the next moment, but what a moment it would be! She pounded away with all her might. When the gigantic nose still didn't move, the princess gave his chin a mighty kick.

"Ouch!" hollered the dragon, and he pulled his head back to rub his jaw with the tip of one wing.

He was probably going to blast her into char now, so she had nothing to lose. She put her hands on her hips and yelled, "Well, this can't be the first time someone has given you a kick!"

"Actually, it is," the dragon whimpered.

"But don't knights and soldiers try to kill you all the time?"

"Of course, but they use swords and spears and build traps and all kinds of nonsense. It never works. The swords are annoying, but they don't really hurt. My skin and armor are very thick and sturdy, except for my poor chin. Usually, I can smell knights coming, and I just fly away. It's all very bothersome. Would you want people following you around and poking you with sticks?"

The princess stared at the dragon, so shocked that she couldn't respond.

Does he really just fly away? she wondered. That logic went against every legend and every story she had ever heard about dragons. Not willing to let her guard down, she saw it as a chance to get rid of him for good.

"Well, I want you to fly away now. Fly out of my kingdom and never come back," the princess demanded, stamping her foot.

"Where am I supposed to go?" the dragon asked quietly. "Everywhere I have been, everywhere I go, there's always someone who wants to kill me. No one will ever let me be."

The dragon seemed sad as he sat down with a thud in the field of clover, and the ground vibrated with his weight. His wings slumped behind him, and a tendril of smoke curled from his nose.

Bianca stared at him in stunned silence. She had expected more smoke and fire and threats. A depressed and defeated-looking dragon was confusing.

"All I ever do is maybe have one of their cows for

dinner," he said, "and the whole village will be after me."

"But don't you burn up forests?" Bianca asked.

"That sounds like an awful lot of work." The dragon sighed. "I'm not sure I have enough flame to burn up a whole forest."

"But don't you tear down castles and eat everyone in your path?"

The dragon shrugged.

"I tried it when I was young, like all the other dragons said I was supposed to, but people taste funny and make an awful fuss. And what would be the point of tearing down a perfectly good castle? I mean, why bother? My flames are pretty good for scaring people away. No one has ever stayed put like you did. Sometimes I have to defend myself, but burning stuff up for no good reason is kind of a waste, don't you think?"

The princess, totally bewildered, sat down in the clover too, right in front of the dragon.

"But what about my father and all the knights and soldiers who came after you in this kingdom?"

"Oh, them," the dragon said. "They made such a clanging and clamoring that I just flew away. They kept right on marching. Never even saw me."

"You didn't burn them up?"

"No." His head drooped.

"Then why did you say you did?"

"Well, I never actually said I did. I said that the same thing happened to them as all the other kings and knights and soldiers. Would-be heroes like to make up stories of grand and noble battles against dragons, but usually, I just fly away." He shifted his wings uncomfortably. "But a dragon has to keep up evil appearances, you know, or too many humans will get ideas about being brave and legendary and come hunting for me."

So the beast hadn't killed her father. Or the knights and soldiers. Or much of anyone else, if she could believe his version of the stories.

"Can you read my mind?" she asked. "Witch Barb said you could read people's minds."

"Oh. I don't think so. I've never tried," he admitted. "Think of something, and I'll see if I can."

Bianca imagined the most beautiful butterfly—all orange and black—like one she had seen once from her tower window.

"Are you thinking about a cow?" he asked.

"No," she said with a laugh. "Not even close."

"Oh. Maybe I'm just hungry, and I'm thinking about cows."

So Witch Barb had been wrong. That made Bianca think of the potion again. She found the bottle in her boot pocket and pulled out the cork.

"What about this?" she asked, holding the bottle up toward him. "It's supposed to be dragon repellent. The witch told me it would make you fly away."

Giving it a hesitant sniff, the dragon wrinkled his scaly nose.

"Pee-uu. I certainly wouldn't try to eat anything smelling like that. I guess, in general, it might be helpful against a dragon."

The princess recorked the bottle and tucked it back into her boot. Then the two sat quietly for a few moments.

Finally, the dragon cleared his throat after the awkward silence, and a puff of smoke snuck out of his nostril.

"If you really are a princess, you should go back to your castle where it is safe and cozy," the dragon said. "I'll just move on to another spot until someone else finds me. Maybe they won't pester me, and I can rest for a few days."

The dragon sighed and wrapped his golden wings around his body in a sad embrace.

Before Bianca could answer, Miss Kitty sauntered into the clearing with them, tail held high in the air. Bianca was about to warn the cat to be careful when the dragon let out a squeal.

"Oh, a kitty cat!" he said, reaching down to touch the little white creature with his wing tip.

Miss Kitty sniffed at his talon and then rubbed against it. Bianca guessed that, since she was magical, the cat knew she was in no danger. The little white creature curled up on the dragon's foot and purred happily. It was all very confounding.

As the princess stared at the dragon, the one

everyone said was monstrous and ferocious, she realized he wasn't so terrible after all. He had spent his life having tales told about him, but none of it was true. Yet people believed the stories and refused to see him any other way than as a dangerous, fire-breathing brute.

In a flash of understanding, Bianca realized she knew exactly how he felt. Her whole life, Nanny and her father had told her about how frail and weak and delicate she was. But she had always known it wasn't true. She thought about the ridiculous rumors the fairies had heard about her. As a princess, she herself had become a topic of legends that people believed without questioning.

The dragon was just as misunderstood as she was.

Both of them had spent their lives being told who and what they were, even if they knew it wasn't true at all. And there had been nothing they could do about it.

But that time was past.

Princess Bianca had proved that she was stronger and braver than anyone believed. She had stepped out on her own, and she had actually conquered the dragon. It wasn't how she expected it to happen, but she had still been brave and strong enough to do it alone. Now it was time to help another creature step outside of the shadow of his own false legends as well.

"No," the princess announced, leaping to her feet. "You don't need to move on. I have a better idea."

Chapter 19

Back at the castle, King Dominic and his knights had finally returned from their quest long enough to restock their supplies and check on the castle. Finding the Frail and Delicate Princess Bianca gone was absolutely the last thing they'd expected.

Looking at the note and listening to Nanny's admission that she had not checked on the princess as regularly as she should, King Dominic felt panic rise up in his throat. For thirteen years, he had kept his precious daughter safe. He had sheltered and protected her from harm of any kind. It was beyond his comprehension that Bianca would have left the castle of her own free will.

"This note is a trick!" he said, waving it in front of Nanny's teary face. "Some upstart prince with grand ambitions or vile intentions has carried my daughter off while we were all distracted and worrying about a dragon that doesn't even seem to exist."

Grabbing his sword by the hilt, the king called for his guard. A massive search party was prepared with only hours to spare before the sun set. Unlike the king, his knights didn't really believe someone had kidnapped the girl. And no one held out much hope that such a sheltered princess could survive the night, much less two, in the forest alone. Of course, none were brave enough to say that out loud to the frantic king.

Knights in armor clanged around the courtyard, organizing the troops to either guard or search. Military horses tossed their heads and flared their nostrils, sensing the tension in the air.

Uncle Frederick blubbered and bawled and would not be comforted. If only he had found the note sooner.

Nanny and Cook huddled together and sobbed.

The remaining townspeople cried and prayed for the safety of their dainty little princess and for mercy from the vicious dragon that could arrive to kill them all at any moment.

Then, out of nowhere, their fears were answered. A golden dragon swooped over the castle walls. His massive wingspan darkened the courtyard as horses and knights and townspeople scattered in terror.

"It is here!" a woman screamed, diving under a hay cart.

"All is lost! All is lost!" Nanny sobbed, ducking into the castle doorway with Cook.

King Dominic stood in the middle of the chaos, eyes on the dragon and hand on his sword. He was an honorable king, and he would not desert his people or his castle. Pulling the gleaming metal from its sheath, he prepared for battle.

The mamothsome beast flapped in place over the tallest tower before coming to rest on a ledge nearby, overlooking the courtyard.

Brave knights in armor ran to challenge him. The

king followed them, ready to defend his people to the bitter end. When flame and stones did not immediately come raining down upon them, they looked up to the sky, searching for what would happen next.

What they saw was the greatest shock of all.

Sitting perched atop the dragon's golden-armored back was Princess Bianca.

She had latched the donkey's rope around the beast's neck and was smiling and waving like she had every day from her castle window. Her normally tidy hair blew in the breeze, and her clothes were ill-fitting and wrinkled, but it was still their princess.

Everyone just stood and stared, speechless.

Nanny and Cook peeked out of the doorway.

The knights dropped their swords, and the king fell to his knees.

There wasn't a sound in the courtyard.

"Hello!" Princess Bianca yelled. "Don't worry. I'm fine! My friend the dragon has rescued me from the forest!"

With that, the golden beast unfurled his wings and

glided gracefully down to the courtyard, landing as gently as possible right next to the king. Everyone gasped in wonder as the princess deftly slid down from the mighty dragon's back. She was caught at the last moment by his wing, and then lowered carefully to the ground.

After hugging her astonished father in a tight embrace, the princess told everyone about her meeting with the dragon.

"He won't hurt anyone, Father. I'm sure of it. He just needs a place to call his own."

The dragon lowered his head to meet the princess face-to-face. She patted his nose gently.

"He has agreed to be my protector." Bianca smiled. "And to guard our castle as well."

"You have tamed the dragon?" the king asked in wonder.

She scratched the dragon behind his ear, and he gurgled happily, a puff of smoke escaping from his nose.

"He didn't need to be tamed," she said. "He just needed to be welcomed and appreciated."

Bianca felt a tug on her pants and looked down at a small girl with golden curls.

"Did he really save you?" the girl asked.

"Of course," Bianca said, taking the girl's hand, "and he will keep all of us safe from now on."

Bianca reached up and patted the dragon's golden, scaly chest. He chortled and then puffed giant smoke rings into the air.

"Oooo," the crowd all gasped.

"What's his name?" the little girl asked.

Bianca looked up at the dragon, but he just shook his head.

"No one has ever called me anything but dragon," he admitted sadly. "Well, maybe some other things, but they weren't very nice names."

"I think we should call him Fred," the girl said. "Fred the Dragon."

"Hmmm," Bianca said. "I'm not sure how Uncle Frederick would feel about that." She glanced at her uncle warily, but he was too busy gawking up at the massive beast to notice anything else. "We should probably work on just the perfect name for our new friend. Every good protector needs just the right name."

"Mercy, he's big," Uncle Frederick mumbled.

"Percy?" the dragon said.

"No, he said 'mercy,'" Bianca told him.

"Oh," the dragon said sadly. "I kind of liked Percy."

"If that's what you like, then Percy it will be," she said, smiling up at her new friend.

"Percy the Merciful," the little girl said, daring to reach out and touch the edge of his wing.

"Oh, I do like the sound of that," Percy said with a proud puff of smoke. "You have made me a part of your kingdom, and I will stand guard for you."

"Percy the Merciful, Guardian of the Kingdom of Pacifico." Bianca grinned up at the dragon.

The crowd applauded in agreement.

In response, he sat up tall and spread his wings wide, knocking over two hay carts in the process.

King Dominic finally stepped forward to make the moment official.

“I hereby declare that Percy the Merciful, as this dragon shall henceforth be known, is the official protector of my daughter, Princess Bianca, and my entire kingdom.”

He held Bianca by the shoulders and kissed her on the forehead. Then he looked deeply into her eyes. The king noticed something there he had never seen before. A spark, maybe. As she stood next to him in the bedraggled peasant clothes, her hair windblown and free, he also realized there would be no going back. His daughter would never again be content to hide in a castle tower and wave from the window once a day.

The king also realized there was little chance this young woman would agree to marry the spoiled prince of his choosing. And why should she? Look at what she, his frail and delicate little princess, had accomplished all on her own. At that moment, King Dominic knew his daughter was already prepared to be a wise ruler of his kingdom.

“It is hard to imagine you traveling the forest roads all by yourself,” he said to Bianca. “You found shelter, kept yourself safe, and were brave enough to save us all. I never in a million years thought you could."

Bianca just smiled up at him, grateful he was safe and sound and thrilled to the tips of her toes that he was proud of her.

"It seems we were wrong about both of you," the king said loud enough for all to hear. "We will set aside a place for the dragon to live and will share our food with him, and in return, he will protect our kingdom—and especially my daughter, who has proven she has a more courageous and wise heart than all of us. From now on, Princess Bianca shall be called the Bravest Princess in the World."

The crowd cheered in agreement once more.

Nanny began sobbing again, but this time with tears of joy.

Percy blew a stream of fire into the air that lit up the sky for miles. Then he gazed down adoringly at Bianca.

The princess finished hugging her father and then wrapped her arms around Percy's leg.

The little girl with the golden curls squealed in delight, and Bianca saw Miss Kitty fluttering into the courtyard.

"Oh," the princess said, "she must have followed us home."

Landing on the dragon's shoulder, Miss Kitty sat up tall and proud.

"I think we have a new addition to the family," Bianca said to her father.

"Well, you have always wanted a cat," he admitted with a shrug. "Though I think that creature is a bit of something else as well."

"I think Miss Kitty is part fairy," she said, "like the ones I met in the forest."

"You met fairies?"

"Yes, Father. A blue one, and a green one, and an orange one. They gave me the magical acorn that helped me fight off the wolf in the forest."

"A wolf?" The king's eyes grew wide. "You faced a wolf?"

"Yes. And a witch."

"A witch?" the king gasped.

"Yes. Witch Barb. But she wasn't a bad person at all.

As a matter of fact, she gave me this dragon-repelling potion to keep me safe."

Bianca pulled the bottle from her boot pocket and handed it to her father.

"You met Barbie? She's still alive?"

"Yes, but I guess I really didn't need any dragon repellent after all," she admitted. "Percy, you really should go back and get Sammy, my poor donkey. He's probably still stuck at the riverbank where we spotted him on the way back to the castle."

"Of course, Princess Bianca," the dragon said. "I will make sure he is home before dark. I will carry him gently in my paw."

"And he thought getting on a raft was scary." She laughed, imagining what Sammy's reaction would be when the dragon scooped him up.

Nanny ventured over, not so sure about the giant beast sitting in the courtyard but unable to stay away from her princess any longer.

"Princess Bianca?" she whispered.

"Oh, Nanny!" Bianca grabbed her in a big hug. "I'm so sorry if you were worried about me."

"Well, just a little bit," Nanny said, wiping her face with her white lace hankie.

Bianca smiled, imagining what her devoted Nanny must have put everyone else through while she was gone.

Nanny gasped and jumped back as Miss Kitty fluttered down between them, arcing her descent in a lazy spiral to proudly show off her fancy pink wings.

"Meerrrow," she said, announcing her presence.

Miss Kitty rubbed her head on Bianca's leg. Then she sat down to wash her furry white face with a front paw.

"Gracious me," Nanny said. "What did you find on your journey?"

Bianca leaned over and whispered into her dear lifelong friend's ear.

"Me, Nanny. I found me."

Nanny smiled and hugged her princess—a little harder than she had ever dared.

It certainly wasn't how Bianca had expected her adventure to end when she snuck out of the castle three days earlier. But the dragon had been conquered, in a way. She had not only saved the kingdom but had found a way to protect it for many years to come.

And the words "frail and delicate" were heard no more.

Epilogue

Percy the Merciful was true to his word. He continued to protect the kingdom for Princess Bianca the Brave, and then for Queen Bianca the Strong, and then for her children for generations to come. And anyone who tried to interfere with the Kingdom of Pacifico had Percy to answer to.

But those are stories for another time.

The End

Acknowledgements

Bianca's story has been evolving for decades. It started out as a very brief picture book that I wrote in fifth grade. The illustrations were awful, not much more than stick figures, and the princess kills the dragon for calling her fat (so politically incorrect!), but it won a contest at the University of Illinois. Thank you to my fantastic teacher, Mr. Lenkart, for giving us this assignment and entering the stories.

Because it was a "certificate of merit" winner, someone at the university created puppets for each character and did a puppet show of the story. I have vivid memories of this. I don't remember how many other winners there were. Maybe dozens. All that stood out in my mind was that I had won. During that year of school, I continued writing little sequels to the story and sharing them with friends in class. I credit this as the start of my life as a writer.

This princess story stayed with me through the

years. It even became an adult short story in college during a class on science fiction writing, where the princess saves a prince before she slays the dragon. During the 1990s, I rewrote this story as a detailed picture book. It was easy to imagine lovely illustrations, like the fairy tales published centuries ago. Sadly, publishers disagreed. That is not the style of current picture books. So it sat in my drawer.

But as I began writing a middle-grade series around 2010, the Cats in the Mirror books and their companion stories, I began to wonder about letting my little frail and delicate princess branch out into a chapter book. What kind of adventures could she have on her way to slay the dragon? What if she didn't have to slay him in the end? What if . . . ? I hope you have enjoyed where those what-ifs took me.

As always, I am grateful for the input of my editor, Kathy Lapeyre (http://fictioneditingbykathy.com). The cover design this time was a team effort. My daughter Callista (who did the illustrations for *Max's Wild Night* and *Dottie's Daring Day*) provided the original drawings for Percy the Dragon and Bianca, and Kelsey Rice added the color and style and made it all fantastic and beautiful.

Special thanks need to be lavished on my writing critique group, Ozark Mountain Guild (OMG), for their support and excellent ideas on improving the story and my writing of it. Five pages at a time, twice a month, they nitpicked every little detail. Thank you! Extra gratitude goes to Jennifer Murray-McClain for taking the time to read the final version from beginning to end and giving me her notes, most of which led to some change or another.

And, as always, enormous thanks go to my husband, Scott Dendler, for reading, reviewing, questioning, challenging, and supporting all of my writing.

You can find out about all of my books, social media links, blog, and writing adventures at my website: megdendler.com. Or join my Reader's Group through the sidebar at my website and get quarterly updates about new books, sales, and the real-life dramas of my writing life.

And many thanks to you for reading Bianca's story. Without you, I'd just have to sit around telling stories to my pets. They'd listen, but it's not quite the same.

If you enjoyed Bianca's story, please take a moment to leave a review at Amazon or Goodreads or tell a couple of friends!

About the Author

Meg Dendler has considered herself a writer since she won a picture book contest in fifth grade and entertained her classmates with ongoing sequels for the rest of the year. Beginning serious work as a freelancer in the 1990s while teaching elementary and middle school, Meg has more than one hundred articles in print, including interviews with Kirk Douglas, Sylvester Stallone, and Dwayne "The Rock" Johnson. She has won contests with her short stories and poetry, along with multiple international awards for her best-selling "Cats in the Mirror" alien rescue cat children's book series and the dog adventure companion books. Meg is an editor with Pen-L Publishing and also does freelance editing work for independent and self-publishing authors. She is a proud member of SCBWI.

Meg and her family (including four cats and her dog, Max) live in Arkansas.

Visit her at www.megdendler.com for more information about upcoming books and events and all of Meg's social media links.

Don't miss out on Meg's Cats in the Mirror series!

And the companion dog adventure stories

Also by Meg Welch Dendler

It's hard to get on with your life when you're already dead.

Penny had been stuck in the same diner for decades—ever since she died in 1952. Serving ice cream to those who dropped in on their way to the next level of existence, she helped to ease their transition into The Light. Her afterlife was perfect. But when the ridiculously handsome, bad boy biker Jake Thatcher shows up and becomes stuck as well, Penny rediscovers feelings that she thought had been buried with her body. Was her afterlife really as perfect as she thought?

CPSIA information can be obtained
at www.ICGtesting.com
Printed in the USA
LVHW03s1559100718
583280LV00013B/1152/P

9 780692 920411